K. Middleman

THE GLENCOE LITERATURE LIBRARY

Number the Stars

and Related Readings

 Glencoe
McGraw-Hill

New York, New York   Columbus, Ohio   Woodland Hills, California   Peoria, Illinois

Acknowledgments

Grateful acknowledgment is given authors, publishers, photographers, museums, and agents for permission to reprint the following copyrighted material. Every effort has been made to determine copyright owners. In case of any omissions, the Publisher will be pleased to make suitable acknowledgments in future editions.

NUMBER THE STARS by Lois Lowry. Copyright © 1989 by Lois Lowry. Reprinted by permission of Houghton Mifflin Company. All rights reserved.

Excerpts from OCTOBER '45: CHILDHOOD MEMORIES OF THE WAR, copyright © 1955 by Jean-Louis Besson; English translation copyright © 1995 by The Creative Company, reprinted by permission of Harcourt Brace & Company.

Text excerpt "Night of Fire at Berlin Railroad Station" from THE LAST SUNRISE: A True Story by Harold Gordon, copyright © 1989 by Harold Gordon. Reprinted by permission.

"Civilized Denmark," by Garrison Keillor. Copyright © 1998 by Garrison Keillor. Reprinted by permission of Garrison Keillor.

"We Will Be the World" by Sasha Whyte from NEWSWEEK January 8, 1996. All rights reserved. Reprinted by permission.

Text excerpt "Petey and Yotsee and Mario, July 14, 1956" by Henry Roth, copyright © 1956 and renewed. Originally published in *The New Yorker* magazine. Reprinted by permission of the Roslyn Targ Literary Agency, Inc., New York.

Cover Art: Leeds, City Art Galleries
Cover Photo: AKG London

Glencoe/McGraw-Hill

*A Division of The **McGraw·Hill** Companies*

Send all inquiries to:
Glencoe/McGraw-Hill
8787 Orion Place
Columbus, OH 43240

ISBN 0-02-818015-1
Printed in the United States of America
5 6 7 8 9 026 04 03

Contents

Number the Stars

Chapter 1	Why Are You Running?	**1**
Chapter 2	Who Is the Man Who Rides Past?	**7**
Chapter 3	Where is Mrs. Hirsch?	**11**
Chapter 4	It Will Be a Long Night	**17**
Chapter 5	Who Is the Dark-Haired One?	**24**
Chapter 6	Is the Weather Good for Fishing?	**31**
Chapter 7	The House by the Sea	**37**
Chapter 8	There Has Been a Death	**41**
Chapter 9	Why Are You Lying?	**45**
Chapter 10	Let Us Open the Casket	**50**
Chapter 11	Will We See You Again Soon, Peter?	**54**
Chapter 12	Where Was Mama?	**58**
Chapter 13	Run! As Fast As You Can!	**61**
Chapter 14	On the Dark Path	**64**
Chapter 15	My Dogs Smell Meat!	**68**
Chapter 16	I Will Tell You Just a Little	**72**
Chapter 17	All This Long Time	**77**
	Afterword	**80**

Continued

Related Readings 83

Jean-Louis Besson   from *October '45: Childhood Memories of the War*   **personal narrative**   **85**

Harold Gordon   Night of Fire at Berlin Railroad Station   **personal narrative**   **90**

Garrison Keillor   Civilized Denmark   **essay**   **96**

Sasha Whyte   We Will Be the World   **magazine article**   **106**

Henry Roth   Petey and Yotsee and Mario, July 14, 1956   **short story**   **109**

Number
the Stars

Lois Lowry

Chapter 1 | Why Are You Running?

I'LL RACE YOU TO THE CORNER, ELLEN!" Annemarie adjusted the thick leather pack on her back so that her schoolbooks balanced evenly. "Ready?" She looked at her best friend.

Ellen made a face. "No," she said, laughing. "You know I can't beat you—my legs aren't as long. Can't we just walk, like civilized people?" She was a stocky ten-year-old, unlike lanky Annemarie.

"We have to practice for the athletic meet on Friday—I *know* I'm going to win the girls' race this week. I was second last week, but I've been practicing every day. Come on, Ellen," Annemarie pleaded, eyeing the distance to the next corner of the Copenhagen street. "Please?"

Ellen hesitated, then nodded and shifted her own rucksack of books against her shoulders. "Oh, all right. Ready," she said.

"Go!" shouted Annemarie, and the two girls were off, racing along the residential sidewalk. Annemarie's silvery blond hair flew behind her, and Ellen's dark pigtails bounced against her shoulders.

"Wait for me!" wailed little Kirsti, left behind, but the two older girls weren't listening.

Annemarie outdistanced her friend quickly, even though one of her shoes came untied as she sped along the street called Østerbrogade, past the small shops and cafés of her neighborhood here in northeast Copenhagen. Laughing, she skirted an elderly lady in black who carried a shopping bag made of string. A young woman pushing a baby in a carriage moved aside to make way. The corner was just ahead.

Annemarie looked up, panting, just as she reached the corner. Her laughter stopped. Her heart seemed to skip a beat.

"*Halte!*" the soldier ordered in a stern voice.

The German word was as familiar as it was frightening. Annemarie had heard it often enough before, but it had never been directed at her until now.

Behind her, Ellen also slowed and stopped. Far back, little Kirsti was plodding along, her face in a pout because the girls hadn't waited for her.

Annemarie stared up. There were two of them. That meant two helmets, two sets of cold eyes glaring at her, and four tall shiny boots planted firmly on the sidewalk, blocking her path to home.

And it meant two rifles, gripped in the hands of the soldiers. She stared at the rifles first. Then, finally, she looked into the face of the soldier who had ordered her to halt.

"Why are you running?" the harsh voice asked. His Danish was very poor. Three years, Annemarie thought with contempt. Three years they've been in our country, and still they can't speak our language.

"I was racing with my friend," she answered politely. "We have races at school every Friday, and I want to do well, so I—" Her voice trailed away, the sentence unfinished. Don't talk so much, she told herself. Just answer them, that's all.

She glanced back. Ellen was motionless on the sidewalk, a few yards behind her. Farther back, Kirsti was still sulking, and walking slowly toward the corner. Nearby, a woman had come to the doorway of a shop and was standing silently, watching.

One of the soldiers, the taller one, moved toward her. Annemarie recognized him as the one she and Ellen always called, in whispers, "the Giraffe" because of his height and the long neck that extended from his stiff collar. He and his partner were always on this corner.

He prodded the corner of her backpack with the stock of his rifle. Annemarie trembled. "What is in here?" he asked loudly. From the corner of her eye, she saw the shopkeeper move quietly back into the shadows of the doorway, out of sight.

"Schoolbooks," she answered truthfully.

"Are you a good student?" the soldier asked. He seemed to be sneering.

"Yes."

"What is your name?"

"Annemarie Johansen."

"Your friend—is she a good student, too?" He was looking beyond her, at Ellen, who hadn't moved.

Annemarie looked back, too, and saw that Ellen's face, usually rosy-cheeked, was pale, and her dark eyes were wide.

She nodded at the soldier. "Better than me," she said.

"What is her name?"

"Ellen."

"And who is this?" he asked, looking to Annemarie's side. Kirsti had appeared there suddenly, scowling at everyone.

"My little sister." She reached down for Kirsti's hand, but Kirsti, always stubborn, refused it and put her hands on her hips defiantly.

The soldier reached down and stroked her little sister's short, tangled curls. Stand still, Kirsti, Annemarie ordered silently, praying that somehow the obstinate five-year-old would receive the message.

But Kirsti reached up and pushed the soldier's hand away. "*Don't,*" she said loudly.

Both soldiers began to laugh. They spoke to each other in rapid German that Annemarie couldn't understand.

"She is pretty, like my own little girl," the tall one said in a more pleasant voice.

Annemarie tried to smile politely.

"Go home, all of you. Go study your schoolbooks. And don't run. You look like hoodlums when you run."

The two soldiers turned away. Quickly Annemarie reached down again and grabbed her sister's hand before Kirsti could resist. Hurrying the little girl along, she rounded the corner. In a moment Ellen was beside her. They walked quickly, not speaking, with Kirsti between them, toward the large apartment building where both families lived.

When they were almost home, Ellen whispered suddenly, "I was so scared."

"Me too," Annemarie whispered back.

As they turned to enter their building, both girls looked straight ahead, toward the door. They did it purposely so that they would not catch the eyes or the attention of two more soldiers, who stood with their guns on this corner as well. Kirsti scurried ahead of them through the door, chattering about the picture she was bringing home from kindergarten to show Mama. For Kirsti, the soldiers were simply part of the landscape, something that had always been there, on every corner, as unimportant as lampposts, throughout her remembered life.

"Are you going to tell your mother?" Ellen asked Annemarie as they trudged together up the stairs. "I'm not. My mother would be upset."

She said goodbye to Ellen on the second floor, where Ellen lived, and continued on to the third, practicing in her mind a cheerful greeting for her mother: a smile, a description of today's spelling test, in which she had done well.

But she was too late. Kirsti had gotten there first.

"And he poked Annemarie's book bag with his gun, and then he grabbed my hair!" Kirsti was chattering as she took off her sweater in the center of the apartment living room. "But I wasn't scared. Annemarie was, and Ellen, too. But not me!"

Mrs. Johansen rose quickly from the chair by the window where she'd been sitting. Mrs. Rosen, Ellen's mother, was there, too, in the opposite chair. They'd been having coffee together, as they did many afternoons. Of course it wasn't really coffee, though the mothers still called it that: "having coffee." There had been no real coffee in Copenhagen since the beginning of the Nazi occupation. Not even any real tea. The mothers sipped at hot water flavored with herbs.

"Annemarie, what happened? What is Kirsti talking about?" her mother asked anxiously.

"Where's Ellen?" Mrs. Rosen had a frightened look.

"Ellen's in your apartment. She didn't realize you were here," Annemarie explained. "Don't worry. It wasn't anything. It was the two soldiers who stand on the corner of Østerbrogade—you've seen them; you know the tall one with the long neck, the one who looks like a silly giraffe?" She told her mother and Mrs. Rosen of the incident, trying to make it sound humorous and unimportant. But their uneasy looks didn't change.

"I slapped his hand and shouted at him," Kirsti announced importantly.

"No, she didn't, Mama," Annemarie reassured her mother. "She's exaggerating, as she always does."

Mrs. Johansen moved to the window and looked down to the street below. The Copenhagen neighborhood was quiet; it looked the same as always: people coming and going from the shops, children at play, the soldiers on the corner.

She spoke in a low voice to Ellen's mother. "They must be edgy because of the latest Resistance incidents. Did you read in *De Frie Danske* about the bombings in Hillerød and Nørrebro?"

Although she pretended to be absorbed in unpacking her schoolbooks, Annemarie listened, and she knew what her mother was referring to. *De Frie Danske—The Free Danes*—was an illegal newspaper;

Peter Neilsen brought it to them occasionally, carefully folded and hidden among ordinary books and papers, and Mama always burned it after she and Papa had read it. But Annemarie heard Mama and Papa talk, sometimes at night, about the news they received that way: news of sabotage against the Nazis, bombs hidden and exploded in the factories that produced war materials, and industrial railroad lines damaged so that the goods couldn't be transported.

And she knew what Resistance meant. Papa had explained, when she overheard the word and asked. The Resistance fighters were Danish people—no one knew who, because they were very secret— who were determined to bring harm to the Nazis however they could. They damaged the German trucks and cars, and bombed their factories. They were very brave. Sometimes they were caught and killed.

"I must go and speak to Ellen," Mrs. Rosen said, moving toward the door. "You girls walk a different way to school tomorrow. Promise me, Annemarie. And Ellen will promise, too."

"We will, Mrs. Rosen. But what does it matter? There are German soldiers on every corner."

"They will remember your faces," Mrs. Rosen said, turning in the doorway to the hall. "It is important to be one of the crowd, always. Be one of many. Be sure that they never have reason to remember your face." She disappeared into the hall and closed the door behind her.

"He'll remember *my* face, Mama," Kirsti announced happily, "because he said I look like *his* little girl. He said I was pretty."

"If he has such a pretty little girl, why doesn't he go back to her like a good father?" Mrs. Johansen murmured, stroking Kirsti's cheek. "Why doesn't he go back to his own country?"

"Mama, is there anything to eat?" Annemarie asked, hoping to take her mother's mind away from the soldiers.

"Take some bread. And give a piece to your sister."

"With butter?" Kirsti asked hopefully.

"No butter," her mother replied. "You know that."

Kirsti sighed as Annemarie went to the breadbox in the kitchen. "I wish I could have a cupcake," she said. "A big yellow cupcake, with pink frosting."

Her mother laughed. "For a little girl, you have a long memory," she told Kirsti. "There hasn't been any butter, or sugar for cupcakes, for a long time. A year, at least."

"When will there be cupcakes again?"

"When the war ends," Mrs. Johansen said. She glanced through the window, down to the street corner where the soldiers stood, their faces impassive beneath the metal helmets. "When the soldiers leave."

Chapter 2 | Who Is the Man Who Rides Past?

"TELL ME A STORY, Annemarie," begged Kirsti as she snuggled beside her sister in the big bed they shared. "Tell me a fairy tale."

Annemarie smiled and wrapped her arms around her little sister in the dark. All Danish children grew up familiar with fairy tales. Hans Christian Andersen, the most famous of the tale tellers, had been Danish himself.

"Do you want the one about the little mermaid?" That one had always been Annemarie's own favorite.

But Kirsti said no. "Tell one that starts with a king and a queen. And they have a beautiful daughter."

"All right. Once upon a time there was a king," Annemarie began.

"And a queen," whispered Kirsti. "Don't forget the queen."

"And a queen. They lived together in a wonderful palace, and—"

"Was the palace named Amalienborg?" Kirsti asked sleepily.

"Shhh. Don't keep interrupting or I'll never finish the story. No, it wasn't Amalienborg. It was a pretend palace."

Annemarie talked on, making up a story of a king and queen and their beautiful daughter, Princess Kirsten; she sprinkled her tale with formal balls, fabulous gold-trimmed gowns, and feasts of pink frosted cupcakes, until Kirsti's deep, even breathing told her that her sister was sound asleep.

She stopped, waited for a moment, half expecting Kirsti to murmur "Then what happened?" But Kirsti was still. Annemarie's thoughts turned to the real king, Christian X, and the real palace, Amalienborg, where he lived, in the center of Copenhagen.

How the people of Denmark loved King Christian! He was not like fairy tale kings, who seemed to stand on balconies giving orders to subjects, or who sat on golden thrones demanding to be entertained and looking for suitable husbands for their daughters. King Christian was a real human being, a man with a serious, kind face. She had seen him often, when she was younger. Each morning, he had come from the palace on his horse, Jubilee, and ridden alone through the streets of Copenhagen, greeting his people. Sometimes, when Annemarie was a little girl, her older sister, Lise, had taken her to stand on the sidewalk so that she could wave to King Christian. Sometimes he had waved back to the two of them, and smiled. "Now you are special forever," Lise had told her once, "because you have been greeted by a king."

Annemarie turned her head on the pillow and stared through the partly opened curtains of the window into the dim September night. Thinking of Lise, her solemn, lovely sister, always made her sad.

So she turned her thoughts again to the king, who was still alive, as Lise was not. She remembered a story that Papa had told her, shortly after the war began, shortly after Denmark had surrendered and the soldiers had moved in overnight to take their places on the corners.

One evening, Papa had told her that earlier he was on an errand near his office, standing on the corner waiting to cross the street, when King Christian came by on his morning ride. One of the German soldiers had turned, suddenly, and asked a question of a teenage boy nearby.

"Who is that man who rides past here every morning on his horse?" the German soldier had asked.

Papa said he had smiled to himself, amused that the German soldier did not know. He listened while the boy answered.

"He is our king," the boy told the soldier. "He is the King of Denmark."

"Where is his bodyguard?" the soldier had asked.

"And do you know what the boy said?" Papa had asked Annemarie. She was sitting on his lap. She was little, then, only seven years old. She shook her head, waiting to hear the answer.

"The boy looked right at the soldier, and he said, 'All of Denmark is his bodyguard.'"

Annemarie had shivered. It sounded like a very brave answer. "Is it true, Papa?" she asked. "What the boy said?"

Papa thought for a moment. He always considered questions very carefully before he answered them. "Yes," he said at last. "It is true.

Any Danish citizen would die for King Christian, to protect him."

"You too, Papa?"

"Yes."

"And Mama?"

"Mama too."

Annemarie shivered again. "Then I would too, Papa. If I had to."

They sat silently for a moment. From across the room, Mama watched them, Annemarie and Papa, and she smiled. Mama had been crocheting that evening three years ago: the lacy edging of a pillow-case, part of Lise's trousseau. Her fingers moved rapidly, turning the thin white thread into an intricate narrow border. Lise was a grownup girl of eighteen, then, about to be married to Peter Neilsen. When Lise and Peter married, Mama said, Annemarie and Kirsti would have a brother for the very first time.

"Papa," Annemarie had said, finally, into the silence, "sometimes I wonder why the king wasn't able to protect us. Why didn't he fight the Nazis so that they wouldn't come into Denmark with their guns?"

Papa sighed. "We are such a tiny country," he said. "And they are such an enormous enemy. Our king was wise. He knew how few soldiers Denmark had. He knew that many, many Danish people would die if we fought."

"In Norway they fought," Annemarie pointed out.

Papa nodded. "They fought very fiercely in Norway. They had those huge mountains for the Norwegian soldiers to hide in. Even so, Norway was crushed."

In her mind, Annemarie had pictured Norway as she remembered it from the map at school, up above Denmark. Norway was pink on the school map. She imagined the pink strip of Norway crushed by a fist.

"Are there German soldiers in Norway now, the same as here?"

"Yes," Papa said.

"In Holland, too," Mama added from across the room, "and Belgium and France."

"But not in Sweden!" Annemarie announced, proud that she knew so much about the world. Sweden was blue on the map, and she had *seen* Sweden, even though she had never been there. Standing behind Uncle Henrik's house, north of Copenhagen, she had looked across the water—the part of the North Sea that was called the Kattegat—to the land on the other side. "That is Sweden you are seeing," Uncle Henrik had told her. "You are looking across to another country."

"That's true," Papa had said. "Sweden is still free."

And now, three years later, it was *still* true. But much else had changed. King Christian was getting old, and he had been badly injured last year in a fall from his horse, faithful old Jubilee, who had carried him around Copenhagen so many mornings. For days they thought he would die, and all of Denmark had mourned.

But he hadn't. King Christian X was still alive.

It was Lise who was not. It was her tall, beautiful sister who had died in an accident two weeks before her wedding. In the blue carved trunk in the corner of this bedroom—Annemarie could see its shape even in the dark—were folded Lise's pillowcases with their crocheted edges, her wedding dress with its hand-embroidered neckline, unworn, and the yellow dress that she had worn and danced in, with its full skirt flying, at the party celebrating her engagement to Peter.

Mama and Papa never spoke of Lise. They never opened the trunk. But Annemarie did, from time to time, when she was alone in the apartment; alone, she touched Lise's things gently, remembering her quiet, soft-spoken sister who had looked forward so to marriage and children of her own.

Redheaded Peter, her sister's fiancé, had not married anyone in the years since Lise's death. He had changed a great deal. Once he had been like a fun-loving older brother to Annemarie and Kirsti, teasing and tickling, always a source of foolishness and pranks. Now he still stopped by the apartment often, and his greetings to the girls were warm and smiling, but he was usually in a hurry, talking quickly to Mama and Papa about things Annemarie didn't understand. He no longer sang the nonsense songs that had once made Annemarie and Kirsti shriek with laughter. And he never lingered anymore.

Papa had changed, too. He seemed much older and very tired, defeated.

The whole world had changed. Only the fairy tales remained the same.

"And they lived happily ever after," Annemarie recited, whispering into the dark, completing the tale for her sister, who slept beside her, one thumb in her mouth.

Chapter 3 | Where Is Mrs. Hirsch?

THE DAYS OF SEPTEMBER PASSED, one after the other, much the same. Annemarie and Ellen walked to school together, and home again, always now taking the longer way, avoiding the tall soldier and his partner. Kirsti dawdled just behind them or scampered ahead, never out of their sight.

The two mothers still had their "coffee" together in the afternoons. They began to knit mittens as the days grew slightly shorter and the first leaves began to fall from the trees, because another winter was coming. Everyone remembered the last one. There was no fuel now for the homes and apartments in Copenhagen, and the winter nights were terribly cold.

Like the other families in their building, the Johansens had opened the old chimney and installed a little stove to use for heat when they could find coal to burn. Mama used it too, sometimes, for cooking, because electricity was rationed now. At night they used candles for light. Sometimes Ellen's father, a teacher, complained in frustration because he couldn't see in the dim light to correct his students' papers.

"Soon we will have to add another blanket to your bed," Mama said one morning as she and Annemarie tidied the bedroom.

"Kirsti and I are lucky to have each other for warmth in the winter," Annemarie said. "Poor Ellen, to have no sisters."

"She will have to snuggle in with her mama and papa when it gets cold," Mama said, smiling.

"I remember when Kirsti slept between you and Papa. She was supposed to stay in her crib, but in the middle of the night she would climb out and get in with you," Annemarie said, smoothing the pillows on the bed. Then she hesitated and glanced at her mother, fearful that she had said the wrong thing, the thing that would bring the pained look to her mother's face. The days when little Kirsti slept in

Mama and Papa's room were the days when Lise and Annemarie shared this bed.

But Mama was laughing quietly. "I remember, too," she said. "Sometimes she wet the bed in the middle of the night!"

"I did not!" Kirsti said haughtily from the bedroom doorway. "I never, *ever* did that!"

Mama, still laughing, knelt and kissed Kirsti on the cheek. "Time to leave for school, girls," she said. She began to button Kirsti's jacket. "Oh, dear," she said, suddenly. "Look. This button has broken right in half. Annemarie, take Kirsti with you, after school, to the little shop where Mrs. Hirsch sells thread and buttons. See if you can buy just one, to match the others on her jacket. I'll give you some kroner—it shouldn't cost very much."

But after school, when the girls stopped at the shop, which had been there as long as Annemarie could remember, they found it closed. There was a new padlock on the door, and a sign. But the sign was in German. They couldn't read the words.

"I wonder if Mrs. Hirsch is sick," Annemarie said as they walked away.

"I saw her Saturday," Ellen said. "She was with her husband and their son. They all looked just fine. Or at least the *parents* looked just fine—the son *always* looks like a horror." She giggled.

Annemarie made a face. The Hirsch family lived in the neighborhood, so they had seen the boy, Samuel, often. He was a tall teenager with thick glasses, stooped shoulders, and unruly hair. He rode a bicycle to school, leaning forward and squinting, wrinkling his nose to nudge his glasses into place. His bicycle had wooden wheels, now that rubber tires weren't available, and it creaked and clattered on the street.

"I think the Hirsches all went on a vacation to the seashore," Kirsti announced.

"And I suppose they took a big basket of pink frosted cupcakes with them," Annemarie said sarcastically to her sister.

"Yes, I suppose they did," Kirsti replied.

Annemarie and Ellen exchanged looks that meant Kirsti is so *dumb*. No one in Copenhagen had taken a vacation at the seashore since the war began. There *were* no pink frosted cupcakes; there hadn't been for months.

Still, Annemarie thought, looking back at the shop before they turned the corner, where was Mrs. Hirsch? The Hirsch family had gone *somewhere*. Whey else would they close the shop?

Mama was troubled when she heard the news. "Are you sure?" she asked several times.

"We can find another button someplace," Annemarie reassured her. "Or we can take one from the bottom of the jacket and move it up. It won't show very much."

But it didn't seem to be the jacket that worried Mama. "Are you sure the sign was in German?" she asked. "Maybe you didn't look carefully."

"Mama, it had a swastika on it."

Her mother turned away with a distracted look. "Annemarie, watch your sister for a few moments. And begin to peel the potatoes for dinner. I'll be right back."

"Where are you going?" Annemarie asked as her mother started for the door.

"I want to talk to Mrs. Rosen."

Puzzled, Annemarie watched her mother leave the apartment. She went to the kitchen and opened the door to the cupboard where the potatoes were kept. Every night, now, it seemed, they had potatoes for dinner. And very little else.

Annemarie was almost asleep when there was a light knock on the bedroom door. Candlelight appeared as the door opened, and her mother stepped in.

"Are you asleep, Annemarie?"

"No. Why? Is something wrong?"

"Nothing's wrong. But I'd like you to get up and come out to the living room. Peter's here. Papa and I want to talk to you."

Annemarie jumped out of bed, and Kirsti grunted in her sleep. Peter! She hadn't seen him in a long time. There was something frightening about his being here at night. Copenhagen had a curfew, and no citizens were allowed out after eight o'clock. It was very dangerous, she knew, for Peter to visit at this time. But she was delighted that he was here. Though his visits were always hurried—they almost seemed secret, somehow, in a way she couldn't quite put her finger on—still, it was a treat to see Peter. It brought back memories of happier times. And her parents loved Peter, too. They said he was like a son.

Barefoot, she ran to the living room and into Peter's arms. He grinned, kissed her cheek, and ruffled her long hair.

"You've grown taller since I saw you last," he told her. "You're all legs!"

Annemarie laughed. "I won the girls' footrace last Friday at school," she told him proudly. "Where have you been? We've missed you!"

"My work takes me all over," Peter explained. "Look, I brought you something. One for Kirsti, too." He reached into his pocket and handed her two seashells.

Annemarie put the smaller one on the table to save it for her sister. She held the other in her hands, turning it in the light, looking at the ridged, pearly surface. It was so like Peter, to bring just the right gift.

"For your mama and papa, I brought something more practical. Two bottles of beer!"

Mama and Papa smiled and raised their glasses. Papa took a sip and wiped the foam from his upper lip. Then his face became more serious.

"Annemarie," he said, "Peter tells us that the Germans have issued orders closing many stores run by Jews."

"Jews?" Annemarie repeated. "Is Mrs. Hirsch Jewish? Is that why the button shop is closed? Why have they done that?"

Peter leaned forward. "It is their way of tormenting. For some reason, they want to torment Jewish people. It has happened in the other countries. They have taken their time here—have let us relax a little. But now it seems to be starting."

"But why the button shop? What harm is a button shop? Mrs. Hirsh is such a nice lady. Even Samuel—he's a dope, but he would never harm anyone. How could he—he can't even see, with his thick glasses!"

Then Annemarie thought of something else. "If they can't sell their buttons, how will they earn a living?"

"Friends will take care of them," Mama said gently. "That's what friends do."

Annemarie nodded. Mama was right, of course. Friends and neighbors would go to the home of the Hirsch family, would take them fish and potatoes and bread and herbs for making tea. Maybe Peter would even take them a beer. They would be comfortable until their shop was allowed to open again.

Then, suddenly, she sat upright, her eyes wide. "Mama!" she said. "Papa! The Rosens are Jewish, too!"

Her parents nodded, their faces serious and drawn. "I talked to Sophy Rosen this afternoon, after you told me about the button shop," Mama said. "She knows what is happening. But she doesn't think that it will affect them."

Annemarie thought, and understood. She relaxed. "Mr. Rosen doesn't have a shop. He's a teacher. They can't close a whole school!" She looked at Peter with the question in her eyes. "Can they?"

"I think the Rosens will be all right," he said. "But you keep an eye on your friend Ellen. And stay away from the soldiers. Your mother told me about what happened on Østerbrogade."

Annemarie shrugged. She had almost forgotten the incident. "It was nothing. They were only bored and looking for someone to talk to, I think."

She turned to her father. "Papa, do you remember what you heard the boy say to the soldier? That all of Denmark would be the king's bodyguard?"

Her father smiled. "I have never forgotten it," he said.

"Well," Annemarie said slowly, "now I think that all of Denmark must be bodyguard for the Jews, as well."

"So we shall be," Papa replied.

Peter stood. "I must go," he said. "And you, Longlegs, it is way past your bedtime now." He hugged Annemarie again.

Later, once more in her bed beside the warm cocoon of her sister, Annemarie remembered how her father had said, three years before, that he would die to protect the king. That her mother would, too. And Annemarie, seven years old, had announced proudly that she also would.

Now she was ten, with long legs and no more silly dreams of pink-frosted cupcakes. And now she—and all the Danes—were to be bodyguard for Ellen, and Ellen's parents, and all of Denmark's Jews.

Would she die to protect them? *Truly?* Annemarie was honest enough to admit, there in the darkness, to herself, that she wasn't sure.

For a moment she felt frightened. But she pulled the blanket up higher around her neck and relaxed. It was all imaginary, anyway—not real. It was only in the fairy tales that people were called upon to be so brave, to die for one another. Not in real-life Denmark. Oh, there were the soldiers; that was true. And the courageous Resistance leaders, who sometimes lost their lives; that was true, too.

But ordinary people like the Rosens and the Johansens? Annemarie admitted to herself, snuggling there in the quiet dark, that she was glad to be an ordinary person who would never be called upon for courage.

Chapter 4 | It Will Be a Long Night

ALONE IN THE APARTMENT while Mama was out shopping with Kirsti, Annemarie and Ellen were sprawled on the living room floor playing with paper dolls. They had cut the dolls from Mama's magazines, old ones she had saved from past years. The paper ladies had old-fashioned hair styles and clothes, and the girls had given them names from Mama's very favorite book. Mama had told Annemarie and Ellen the entire story of *Gone with the Wind,* and the girls thought it much more interesting and romantic than the king-and-queen tales that Kirsti loved.

"Come, Melanie," Annemarie said, walking her doll across the edge of the rug. "Let's dress for the ball."

"All right, Scarlett, I'm coming," Ellen replied in a sophisticated voice. She was a talented performer; she often played the leading roles in school dramatics. Games of the imagination were always fun when Ellen played.

The door opened and Kirsti stomped in, her face tear-stained and glowering. Mama followed her with an exasperated look and set a package down on the table.

"I won't!" Kirsti sputtered. "I won't ever, *ever* wear them! Not if you chain me in a prison and beat me with sticks!"

Annemarie giggled and looked questioningly at her mother. Mrs. Johansen sighed. "I bought Kirsti some new shoes," she explained. "She's outgrown her old ones."

"Goodness, Kirsti," Ellen said, "I wish my mother would get *me* some new shoes. I love new things, and it's so hard to find them in the stores."

"Not if you go to a *fish* store!" Kirsti bellowed. "But most mothers wouldn't make their daughters wear ugly *fish* shoes!"

"Kirsten," Mama said soothingly, "you know it wasn't a fish store. And we were lucky to find shoes at all."

Kirsti sniffed. "Show them," she commanded. "Show Annemarie and Ellen how ugly they are."

Mama opened the package and took out a pair of little girl's shoes. She held them up, and Kirsti looked away in disgust.

"You know there's no leather anymore," Mama explained. "But they've found a way to make shoes out of fish skin. I don't think these are too ugly."

Annemarie and Ellen looked at the fish skin shoes. Annemarie took one in her hand and examined it. It was odd-looking; the fish scales were visible. But it was a shoe, and her sister needed shoes.

"It's not so bad, Kirsti," she said, lying a little.

Ellen turned the other one over in her hand. "You know," she said, "it's only the color that's ugly."

"Green!" Kirsti wailed. "I will never, *ever* wear green shoes!"

"In our apartment," Ellen told her, "my father has a jar of black, black ink. Would you like these shoes better if they were black?"

Kirsti frowned. "Maybe I would," she said, finally.

"Well, then," Ellen told her, "tonight if your mama doesn't mind, I'll take the shoes home and ask my father to make them black for you, with his ink."

Mama laughed. "I think that would be a fine improvement. What do you think, Kirsti?"

Kirsti pondered. "Could he make them shiny?" she asked. "I want them shiny."

Ellen nodded. "I think he could. I think they'll be quite pretty, black and shiny."

Kirsti nodded. "All right, then," she said. "But you mustn't tell anyone that they're *fish*. I don't want anyone to know." She took her new shoes, holding them disdainfully, and put them on a chair. Then she looked with interest at the paper dolls.

"Can I play, too?" Kirsti asked. "Can I have a doll?" She squatted beside Annemarie and Ellen on the floor.

Sometimes, Annemarie thought, Kirsti was such a pest, always butting in. But the apartment was small. There was no other place for Kirsti to play. And if they told her to go away, Mama would scold.

"Here," Annemarie said, and handed her sister a cut-out little girl doll. "We're playing *Gone With the Wind*. Melanie and Scarlett are going to a ball. You can be Bonnie. She's Scarlett's daughter."

Kirsti danced her doll up and down happily. "I'm going to the ball!" she announced in a high, pretend voice.

Ellen giggled. "A little girl wouldn't go to a ball. Let's make them go someplace else. Let's make them go to Tivoli!"

"Tivoli!" Annemarie began to laugh. "That's in Copenhagen! *Gone With the Wind* is in America!"

"Tivoli, Tivoli, Tivoli," little Kirsti sang, twirling her doll in a circle.

"It doesn't matter, because it's only a game anyway," Ellen pointed out. "Tivoli can be over there, by that chair. 'Come, Scarlett,'" she said, using her doll voice, "'we shall go to Tivoli to dance and watch the fireworks, and maybe there will be some handsome men there! Bring your silly daughter Bonnie, and she can ride on the carousel.'"

Annemarie grinned and walked her Scarlett toward the chair that Ellen had designated as Tivoli. She loved Tivoli Gardens, in the heart of Copenhagen; her parents had taken her there, often, when she was a little girl. She remembered the music and the brightly colored lights, the carousel and ice cream and especially the magnificent fireworks in the evenings: the huge colored splashes and bursts of lights in the evening sky.

"I remember the fireworks best of all," she commented to Ellen.

"Me too," Kirsti said. "I remember the fireworks."

"Silly," Annemarie scoffed. "You never saw the fireworks." Tivoli Gardens was closed now. The German occupation forces had burned part of it, perhaps as a way of punishing the fun-loving Danes for their lighthearted pleasures.

Kirsti drew herself up, her small shoulders stiff. "I did too," she said belligerently. "It was my birthday. I woke up in the night and I could hear the booms. And there were lights in the sky. Mama said it was fireworks for my birthday!"

Then Annemarie remembered. Kirsti's birthday was late in August. And that night, only a month before, she, too, had been awakened and frightened by the sound of explosions. Kirsti was right—the sky in the southeast had been ablaze, and Mama had comforted her by calling it a birthday celebration. "Imagine, such fireworks for a little girl five years old!" Mama had said, sitting on their bed, holding the dark curtain aside to look through the window at the lighted sky.

The next evening's newspaper had told the sad truth. The Danes had destroyed their own naval fleet, blowing up the vessels one by one, as the Germans approached to take over the ships for their own use.

"How sad the king must be," Annemrarie had heard Mama say to Papa when they read the news.

"How proud," Papa had replied.

It had made Annemarie feel sad and proud, too, to picture the tall, aging king, perhaps with tears in his blue eyes, as he looked at the remains of his small navy, which now lay submerged and broken in the harbor.

"I don't want to play anymore, Ellen," she said suddenly, and put her paper doll on the table.

"I have to go home, anyway," Ellen said. "I have to help Mama with the housecleaning. Thursday is our New Year. Did you know that?"

"Why is it yours?" asked Kirsti. "Isn't it our New Year, too?"

"No. It's the Jewish New Year. That's just for us. But if you want, Kirsti, you can come that night and watch Mama light the candles."

Annemarie and Kirsti had often been invited to watch Mrs. Rosen light the Sabbath candles on Friday evenings. She covered her head with a cloth and said a special prayer in Hebrew as she did so. Annemarie always stood very quietly, awed, to watch; even Kirsti, usually such a chatterbox, was always still at that time. They didn't understand the words or the meaning, but they could feel what a special time it was for the Rosens.

"Yes," Kirsti agreed happily. "I'll come and watch your mama light the candles, and I'll wear my new black shoes."

But this time was to be different. Leaving for school on Thursday with her sister, Annemarie saw the Rosens walking to the synagogue early in the morning, dressed in their best clothes. She waved to Ellen, who waved happily back.

"Lucky Ellen," Annemarie said to Kirsti. "She doesn't have to go to school today."

"But she probably has to sit very, very still, like we do in church," Kirsti pointed out. "*That's* no fun."

That afternoon, Mrs. Rosen knocked at their door but didn't come inside. Instead, she spoke for a long time in a hurried, tense voice to

Annemarie's mother in the hall. When Mama returned, her face was worried, but her voice was cheerful.

"Girls," she said, "we have a nice surprise. Tonight Ellen will be coming to stay overnight and to be our guest for a few days! It isn't often we have a visitor."

Kirsti clapped her hands in delight.

"But, Mama," Annemarie said, in dismay, "it's their New Year. They were going to have a celebration at home! Ellen told me that her mother managed to get a chicken someplace, and she was going to roast it—their first roast chicken in a year or more!"

"Their plans have changed," Mama said briskly. "Mr. and Mrs. Rosen have been called away to visit some relatives. So Ellen will stay with us. Now, let's get busy and put clean sheets on your bed. Kirsti, you may sleep with Mama and Papa tonight, and we'll let the big girls giggle together by themselves."

Kirsti pouted, and it was clear that she was about to argue. "Mama will tell you a special story tonight," her mother said. "One just for you."

"About a king?" Kirsti asked dubiously.

"About a king, if you wish," Mama replied.

"All right, then. But there must be a queen, too," Kirsti said.

Though Mrs. Rosen had sent her chicken to the Johansens, and Mama made a lovely dinner large enough for second helpings all around, it was not an evening of laughter and talk. Ellen was silent at dinner. She looked frightened. Mama and Papa tried to speak of cheerful things, but it was clear that they were worried, and it made Annemarie worry, too. Only Kirsti was unaware of the quiet tension in the room. Swinging her feet in their newly blackened and shiny shoes, she chattered and giggled during dinner.

"Early bedtime tonight, little one," Mama announced after the dishes were washed. "We need extra time for the long story promised, about the king and queen." She disappeared with Kirsti into the bedroom.

"What's happening?" Annemarie asked when she and Ellen were alone with Papa in the living room. "Something's wrong. What is it?"

Papa's face was troubled. "I wish that I could protect you children from this knowledge," he said quietly. "Ellen, you already know. Now we must tell Annemarie."

He turned to her and stroked her hair with his gentle hand. "This morning, at the synagogue, the rabbi told his congregation that the Nazis have taken the synagogue lists of all the Jews. Where they live, what their names are. Of course the Rosens were on that list, along with many others."

"Why? Why did they want those names?"

"They plan to arrest all the Danish Jews. They plan to take them away. And we have been told that they may come tonight."

"I don't understand! Take them where?"

Her father shook his head. "We don't know where, and we don't really know why. They call it 'relocation.' We don't even know what that means. We only know that it is wrong, and it is dangerous, and we must help."

Annemarie was stunned. She looked at Ellen and saw that her best friend was crying silently.

"Where are Ellen's parents? We must help them, too!"

"We couldn't take all three of them. If the Germans came to search our apartment, it would be clear that the Rosens were here. One person we can hide. Not three. So Peter has helped Ellen's parents to go elsewhere. We don't know where. Ellen doesn't know either. But they are safe."

Ellen sobbed aloud, and put her face in her hands. Papa put his arm around her. "They are safe, Ellen. I promise you that. You will see them again quite soon. Can you try hard to believe my promise?"

Ellen hesitated, nodded, and wiped her eyes with her hand.

"But, Papa," Annemarie said, looking around the small apartment, with its few pieces of furniture: the fat stuffed sofa, the table and chairs, the small bookcase against the wall. "You said that we would hide her. How can we do that? Where can she hide?"

Papa smiled. "That part is easy. It will be as your mama said: you two will sleep together in your bed, and you may giggle and talk and tell secrets to each other. And if anyone comes—"

Ellen interrupted him. "Who might come? Will it be soldiers? Like the ones on the corners?" Annemarie remembered how terrified Ellen had looked the day when the soldier had questioned them on the corner.

"I really don't think anyone will. But it never hurts to be prepared. If anyone should come, even soldiers, you two will be sisters. You are together so much, it will be easy for you to pretend that you are sisters."

He rose and walked to the window. He pulled the lace curtain aside and looked down into the street. Outside, it was beginning to grow dark. Soon they would have to draw the black curtains that all Danes had on their windows; the entire city had to be completely darkened at night. In a nearby tree, a bird was singing; otherwise it was quiet. It was the last night of September.

"Go, now, and get into your nightgowns. It will be a long night."

Annemarie and Ellen got to their feet. Papa suddenly crossed the room and put his arms around them both. He kissed the top of each head: Annemarie's blond one, which reached to his shoulder, and Ellen's dark hair, the thick curls braided as always into pigtails.

"Don't be frightened," he said to them softly. "Once I had three daughters. Tonight I am proud to have three daughters again."

Chapter 5

Who Is the Dark-Haired One?

Do you really think anyone will come?" Ellen asked nervously, turning to Annemarie in the bedroom. "Your father doesn't think so."

"Of course not. They're always threatening stuff. They just like to scare people." Annemarie took her nightgown from a hook in the closet.

"Anyway, if they did, it would give me a chance to practice acting. I'd just pretend to be Lise. I wish I were taller, though," Ellen stood on tiptoe, trying to make herself tall. She laughed at herself, and her voice was more relaxed.

"You were great as the Dark Queen in the school play last year," Annemarie told her. "You should be an actress when you grow up."

"My father wants me to be a teacher. He wants *everyone* to be a teacher, like him. But maybe I could convince him that I should go to acting school." Ellen stood on tiptoe again, and made an imperious gesture with her arm. "I am the Dark Queen," she intoned dramatically. "I have come to command the night!"

"You should try saying, 'I am Lise Johansen!'" Annemarie said, grinning. "If you told the Nazis that you were the Dark Queen, they'd hall you off to a mental institution."

Ellen dropped her actress pose and sat down, with her legs curled under her, on the bed. "They won't really come here, do you think?" she asked again.

Annemarie shook her head. "Not in a million years." She picked up her hairbrush.

The girls found themselves whispering as they got ready for bed. There was no need, really, to whisper; they were, after all, supposed to be normal sisters and Papa had said they could giggle and talk. The bedroom door was closed.

But the night did seem, somehow, different from a normal night. And so they whispered.

"How did your sister die, Annemarie?" Ellen asked suddenly. "I remember when it happened. And I remember the funeral—it was the only time I have ever been in a Lutheran church. But I never knew just what happened."

"I don't know *exactly*," Annemarie confessed. "She and Peter were out somewhere together, and then there was a telephone call, that there had been an accident. Mama and Papa rushed to the hospital—remember, your mother came and stayed with me and Kirsti? Kirsti was already asleep and she slept right through everything, she was so little then. But I stayed up, and I was with your mother in the living room when my parents came home in the middle of the night. And they told me Lise had died."

"I remember it was raining," Ellen said sadly. "It was still raining the next morning when Mama told me. Mama was crying, and the rain made it seem as if the whole *world* was crying."

Annemarie finished brushing her long hair and handed her hairbrush to her best friend. Ellen undid her braids, lifted her dark hair away from the thin gold chain she wore around her neck—the chain that held the Star of David—and began to brush her thick curls.

"I think it was partly because of the rain. They said she was hit by a car. I suppose the streets were slippery, and it was getting dark, and maybe the driver just couldn't see," Annemarie went on, remembering. "Papa looked so angry. He made one hand into a fist, and he kept pounding it into the other hand. I remember the noise of it: slam, slam, slam."

Together they got into the wide bed and pulled up the covers. Annemarie blew out the candle and drew the dark curtains aside so that the open window near the bed let in some air. "See that blue trunk in the corner?" she said, pointing through the darkness. "Lots of Lise's things are in there. Even her wedding dress. Mama and Papa have never looked at those things, not since the day they packed them away."

Ellen sighed. "She would have looked so beautiful in her wedding dress. She had such a pretty smile. I used to pretend that she was *my* sister, too."

"She would have liked that," Annemarie told her. "She loved you."

"That's the worst thing in the world," Ellen whispered. "To be dead so young. I wouldn't want the Germans to take my family away—to make us live someplace else. But still, it wouldn't be so bad as being dead."

Annemarie leaned over and hugged her. "They won't take you away," she said. "Not your parents, either. Papa promised that they were safe, and he always keeps his promises. And you are quite safe, here with us."

For a while they continued to murmur in the dark, but the murmurs were interrupted by yawns. Then Ellen's voice stopped, she turned over, and in a minute her breathing was quiet and slow.

Annemarie stared at the window where the sky was outlined and a tree branch moved slightly in the breeze. Everything seemed very familiar, very comforting. Dangers were no more than odd imaginings, like ghost stories that children made up to frighten one another: things that couldn't possibly happen. Annemarie felt completely safe here in her own home, with her parents in the next room and her best friend asleep beside her. She yawned contentedly and closed her eyes.

It was hours later, but still dark, when she was awakened abruptly by the pounding on the apartment door.

Annemarie eased the bedroom door open quietly, only a crack, and peeked out. Behind her, Ellen was sitting up, her eyes wide.

She could see Mama and Papa in their nightclothes, moving about. Mama held a lighted candle, but as Annemarie watched, she went to a lamp and switched it on. It was so long a time since they had dared to use the strictly rationed electricity after dark that the light in the room seemed startling to Annemarie, watching through the slightly opened bedroom door. She saw her mother look automatically to the blackout curtains, making certain that they were tightly drawn.

Papa opened the front door to the soldiers.

"This is the Johansen apartment?" A deep voice asked the question loudly, in the terribly accented Danish.

"Our name is on the door, and I see you have a flashlight," Papa answered. "What do you want? Is something wrong?"

"I understand you are a friend of your neighbors the Rosens, Mrs. Johansen," the soldier said angrily.

"Sophy Rosen is my friend, that is true," Mama said quietly. "Please, could you speak more softly? My children are asleep."

"Then you will be so kind as to tell me where the Rosens are." He made no effort to lower his voice.

"I assume they are at home, sleeping. It is four in the morning, after all," Mama said.

Annemarie heard the soldier stalk across the living room toward the kitchen. From her hiding place in the narrow sliver of open doorway, she could see the heavy uniformed man, a holstered pistol at his waist, in the entrance to the kitchen, peering in toward the sink.

Another German voice said, "The Rosens' apartment is empty. We are wondering if they might be visiting their good friends the Johansens."

"Well," said Papa, moving slightly so that he was standing in front of Annemarie's bedroom door, and she could see nothing except the dark blur of his back, "as you see, you are mistaken. There is no one here but my family."

"You will not object if we look around." The voice was harsh, and it was not a question.

"It seems we have no choice," Papa replied.

"Please don't wake my children," Mama requested again. "There is no need to frighten little ones."

The heavy, booted feet moved across the floor and into the other bedroom. A closet door opened and closed with a bang.

Annemarie eased her bedroom door closed silently. She stumbled through the darkness to the bed.

"Ellen," she whispered urgently, "take your necklace off!"

Ellen's hands flew to her neck. Desperately she began trying to unhook the tiny clasp. Outside the bedroom door, the harsh voices and heavy footsteps continued.

"I can't get it open!" Ellen said frantically. "I never take it off— I can't even remember how to open it!"

Annemarie heard a voice just outside the door. "What is here?"

"Shhh," her mother replied. "My daughters' bedroom. They are sound asleep."

"Hold still," Annemarie commanded. "This will hurt." She grabbed the little gold chain, yanked with all her strength, and broke it. As the door opened and light flooded into the bedroom, she crumpled it into her hand and closed her fingers tightly.

Terrified, both girls looked up at the three Nazi officers who entered the room.

One of the men aimed a flashlight around the bedroom. He went to the closet and looked inside. Then with a sweep of his gloved hand he pushed to the floor several coats and a bathrobe that hung from pegs on the wall.

There was nothing else in the room except a chest of drawers, the blue decorated trunk in the corner, and a heap of Kirsti's dolls piled in a small rocking chair. The flashlight beam touched each thing in turn. Angrily the officer turned toward the bed.

"Get up!" he ordered. "Come out here!"

Trembling, the two girls rose from the bed and followed him, brushing past the two remaining officers in the doorway, to the living room.

Annemarie looked around. These three uniformed men were different from the ones on the street corners. The street soldiers were often young, sometimes ill at ease, and Annemarie remembered how the Giraffe had, for a moment, let his harsh pose slip and had smiled at Kirsti.

But these men were older and their faces were set with anger.

Her parents were standing beside each other, their faces tense, but Kirsti was nowhere in sight. Thank goodness that Kirsti slept through almost everything. If they had wakened her, she would be wailing—or worse, she would be angry, and her fists would fly.

"Your names?" the officer barked.

"Annemarie Johansen. And this is my sister—"

"Quiet! Let her speak for herself. Your name?" He was glaring at Ellen.

Ellen swallowed. "Lise," she said, and cleared her throat. "Lise Johansen."

The officer stared at them grimly.

"Now," Mama said in a strong voice, "you have seen that we are not hiding anything. May my children go back to bed?"

The officer ignored her. Suddenly he grabbed a handful of Ellen's hair. Ellen winced.

He laughed scornfully. "You have a blond child sleeping in the other room. And you have this blond daughter—" he gestured toward Annemarie with his head. "Where did you get the dark-haired one?"

He twisted the lock of Ellen's hair. "From a different father? From the milkman?"

Papa stepped forward. "Don't speak to my wife in such a way. Let go of my daughter or I will report you for such treatment."

"Or maybe you got her someplace else?" the officer continued with a sneer. "From the Rosens?"

For a moment no one spoke. Then Annemarie, watching in panic, saw her father move swiftly to the small bookcase and take out a book. She saw that he was holding the family photograph album. Very quickly he searched through its pages, found what he was looking for, and tore out three pictures from three separate pages.

He handed them to the German officer, who released Ellen's hair.

"You will see each of my daughters, each with her name written on the photograph," Papa said.

Annemarie knew instantly which photographs he had chosen. The album had many snapshots—all the poorly focused pictures of school events and birthday parties. But it also contained a portrait taken by a photographer, of each girl as a tiny infant. Mama had written, in her delicate handwriting, the name of each baby daughter across the bottom of those photographs.

She realized too, with an icy feeling, why Papa had torn them from the book. At the bottom of each page, below the photograph itself, was written the date. And the real Lise Johansen had been born twenty-one years earlier.

"Kirsten Elisabeth," the officer read, looking at Kirsti's baby picture. He let the photograph fall to the floor.

"Annemarie," he read next, glanced at her, and dropped the second photograph.

"Lise Margrete," he read finally, and stared at Ellen for a long, unwavering moment. In her mind, Annemarie pictured the photograph that he held: the baby, wide-eyed, propped against a pillow, her tiny hand holding a silver teething ring, her bare feet visible below the hem of an embroidered dress. The wispy curls. Dark.

The officer tore the photograph in half and dropped the pieces on the floor. Then he turned, the heels of his shiny boots grinding into the pictures, and left the apartment. Without a word, the other two officers followed. Papa stepped forward and closed the door behind him.

Annemarie relaxed the clenched fingers of her right hand, which still clutched Ellen's necklace. She looked down, and saw that she had imprinted the Star of David into her palm.

Chapter 6 | Is the Weather Good for Fishing?

WE MUST THINK what to do," Papa said. "They are suspicious, now. To be honest, I thought that if they came here at all—and I hoped they wouldn't—that they would just glance around, see that we had no place to hide anyone, and would go away."

"I'm sorry I have dark hair," Ellen murmured. "It made them suspicious."

Mama reached over quickly and took Ellen's hand. "You have beautiful hair, Ellen, just like your mama's," she said. "Don't ever be sorry for that. Weren't we lucky that Papa thought so quickly and found the pictures? And weren't we lucky that Lise had dark hair when she was a baby? It turned blond later on, when she was two or so."

"In between," Papa added, "she was bald for a while!"

Ellen and Annemarie both smiled tentatively. For a moment their fear was eased.

Tonight was the first time, Annemarie realized suddenly, that Mama and Papa had spoken of Lise. The first time in three years.

Outside, the sky was beginning to lighten. Mrs. Johansen went to the kitchen and began to make tea.

"I've never been up so early before," Annemarie said. "Ellen and I will probably fall asleep in school today!"

Papa rubbed his chin for a moment, thinking. "I think we must not take the risk of sending you to school today," he said. "It is possible that they will look for the Jewish children in the schools."

"Not go to school?" Ellen asked in amazement. "My parents have always told me that education is the most important thing. Whatever happens, I must get an education."

"This will only be a vacation, Ellen. For now, your safety is the most important thing. I'm sure your parents would agree. Inge?" Papa called Mama in the kitchen, and she came to the doorway with a teacup in her hand and a questioning look on her face.

"Yes?"

"We must take the girls to Henrik's. You remember what Peter told us. I think today is the day to go to your brother's."

Mrs. Johansen nodded. "I think you are right. But I will take them. You must stay here."

"Stay here and let you go alone? Of course not. I wouldn't send you on a dangerous trip alone."

Mama put a hand on Papa's arm. "If only I go with the girls, it will be safer. They are unlikely to suspect a woman and her children. But if they are watching us—if they see all of us leave? If they are aware that the apartment is empty, that you don't go to your office this morning? Then they will know. Then it will be dangerous. I am not afraid to go alone."

It was very seldom that Mama disagreed with Papa. Annemarie watched his face and knew that he was struggling with the decision. Finally he nodded, reluctantly.

"I will pack some things," Mama said. "What time is it?"

Papa looked at his watch. "Almost five," he said.

"Henrik will still be there. He leaves around five. Why don't you call him?"

Papa went to the telephone. Ellen looked puzzled. "Who is Henrik? Where does he go at five in the morning?" she asked.

Annemarie laughed. "He's my uncle —my mother's brother. And he's a fisherman. They leave very early, all the fishermen, each morning—their boats go out at sunrise."

"Oh, Ellen," she went on. "You will love it there. It is where my grandparents lived, where Mama and Uncle Henrik grew up. It is so beautiful—right on the water. You can stand at the edge of the meadow and look across to Sweden!"

She listened while Papa spoke on the telephone to Uncle Henrik, telling him that Mama and the children were coming for a visit. Ellen had gone into the bathroom and closed the door; Mama was still in the kitchen. So only Annemarie was listening.

It was a very puzzling conversation.

"So, Henrik, is the weather good for fishing?" Papa asked cheerfully, and listened briefly.

Then he continued, "I'm sending Inge to you today with the children, and she will be bringing you a carton of cigarettes.

"Yes, just one," he said, after a moment. Annemarie couldn't hear Uncle Henrik's words. "But there are a lot of cigarettes available in Copenhagen now, if you know where to look," he went on, "and so there will be others coming to you as well, I'm sure."

But it wasn't true. Annemarie was quite certain it wasn't true. Cigarettes were the thing that Papa missed, the way Mama missed coffee. He complained often—he had complained only yesterday—that there were no cigarettes in the stores. The men in his office, he said, making a face, smoked almost anything: sometimes dried weeds rolled in paper, and the smell was terrible.

Why was Papa speaking that way, almost as if he were speaking in code? What was Mama *really* taking to Uncle Henrik?

Then she knew. It was Ellen.

*

The train ride north along the Danish coast was very beautiful. Again and again they could see the sea from the windows. Annemarie had made this trip often to visit her grandparents when they were alive, and later, after they were gone, to see the cheerful, suntanned, unmarried uncle whom she loved.

But the trip was new to Ellen, who sat with her face pressed to the window, watching the lovely homes along the seaside, the small farms and villages.

"Look!" Annemarie exclaimed, and pointed to the opposite side. "It's Klampenborg, and the Deer Park! Oh, I wish we could stop here, just for a little while!"

Mama shook her head. "Not today," she said. The train did stop at the small Klampenborg station, but none of the few passengers got off. "Have you ever been there, Ellen?" Mama asked, but Ellen said no.

"Well, someday you will go. Someday you will walk through the park and you will see hundreds of deer, tame and free."

Kirsti wriggled to her knees and peered through the window. "I don't see any deer!" she complained.

"They are there, I'm sure," Mama told her. "They're hiding in the trees."

The train started again. The door at the end of their car opened and two German soldiers appeared. Annemarie tensed. Not here, on the train, too? They were *everywhere*.

Together the soldiers strolled through the car, glancing at passengers, stopping here and there to ask a question. One of them had something stuck in his teeth; he probed with his tongue and distorted his own face. Annemarie watched with a kind of frightened fascination as the pair approached.

One of the soldiers looked down with a bored expression on his face. "Where are you going?" he asked.

"Gilleleje," Mama replied calmly. "My brother lives there. We are going to visit him."

The soldiers turned away and Annemarie relaxed. Then, without warning, he turned back. "Are you visiting your brother for the New Year?" he asked suddenly.

Mama stared at him with a puzzled look. "New Year?" she asked. "It is only October."

"And guess what!" Kirsti exclaimed suddenly, in a loud voice, looking at the soldier.

Annemarie's heart sank and she looked at her mother. Mama's eyes were frightened. "Shhh, Kirsti," Mama said. "Don't chatter so."

But Kirsti paid no attention to Mama, as usual. She looked cheerfully at the soldier, and Annemarie knew what she was about to say: This is our friend Ellen and it's *her* New Year.

But she didn't. Instead, Kirsti pointed at her feet. "I'm going to visit my Uncle Henrik," she chirped, "and I'm wearing my brand-new shiny black shoes!"

The soldier chuckled and moved on.

Annemarie gazed through the window again. The trees, the Baltic Sea, and the cloudy October sky passed in a blur as they continued north along the coast.

"Smell the air," Mama said when they stepped off the train and made their way to the narrow street. "Isn't it lovely and fresh? It always brings back memories for me."

The air was breezy and cool, and carried the sharp, not unpleasant smell of salt and fish. High against the pale clouds, seagulls soared and cried out as if they were mourning.

Mama looked at her watch. "I wonder if Henrik will be back yet.

But it doesn't matter. The house is always unlocked. Come on, girls, we'll walk. It isn't far, just a little under two miles. And it's a nice day. We'll take the path through the woods instead of the road. It's a little longer, but it's so pretty."

"Didn't you love the castle when we went through Helsingør, Ellen?" Kirsti asked. She had been talking about Kronborg Castle ever since they had seen it, sprawling massive and ancient, beside the sea, from the train. "I wish we could have stopped to visit the castle. Kings live there. And queens."

Annemarie sighed in exasperation with her little sister. "They do not," she said. "They did in the old days. But there aren't any kings there now. Denmark only *has* one king, anyway. And he lives in Copenhagen."

But Kirsti had pranced away, skipping along the sidewalk. "Kings and queens," she sang happily. "Kings and queens."

Mama shrugged and smiled. "Let her dream, Annemarie. I did the same when I was her age."

She turned, leading the way along a tiny, twisting street, heading toward the outskirts of the village. "Things have hardly changed here since I was a girl," she said. "My Aunt Gitte lived there, in that house"—she pointed—"and she's been dead for years. But the house is the same. She always had wonderful flowers in her garden." She peered over the low stone wall and looked at the few flowering bushes as they passed the house. "Maybe they still do, but it's the wrong time of year—there are just those few chrysanthemums left.

"And see, over there?" She pointed again. "My best friend—her name was Helena — lived in that house. Sometimes I used to spend the night with her. But more often she came to my house, on weekends. It was more fun to be in the country.

"My brother Henrik always teased us, though," she continued with a chuckle. "He told us ghost stories and scared us half to death."

The sidewalk ended and Mama turned onto a dirt path bordered by trees. "When I walked each morning into town for school," she said, "my dog followed me this far. At the end of the path he turned and went back home. I guess he was a country dog and didn't like town.

"And do you know what?" she went on, smiling. "I had named him Trofast—Faithful. And it was just the right name for him, because what a faithful dog he was! Every afternoon he was always right here, waiting for me to return. He knew the right time, somehow. Sometimes, as I come around this bend, even today, I feel as if I might come upon Trofast, waiting still, with his tail wagging."

But the path was empty today. No people. No faithful dogs. Mama shifted the bag she was carrying from one hand to the other, and they walked on through the woods until the path opened to a meadow dotted with cows. Here the path skirted the edge of the field, along a fence, and beyond it they could see the gray sea, ruffled by wind. The breeze moved the high grass.

At the end of the pasture, they entered the woods again and Annemarie knew they would soon be there. Uncle Henrik's house was in a clearing beyond these woods.

"Do you mind if I run ahead?" she asked suddenly. "I want to be the first to see the house!"

"Go on," Mama told her. "Run ahead and tell the house we've come home."

Then she put her arm around Ellen's shoulder and added, "Say that we've brought a friend."

Chapter 7	# The House by the Sea

"Oᴴ, Aɴɴᴇᴍᴀʀɪᴇ," Eʟʟᴇɴ sᴀɪᴅ, with awe in her voice, "it is beautiful."

Annemarie looked around and nodded her head in agreement. The house and the meadows that surrounded it were so much a part of her childhood, a part of her life, that she didn't often look at them with fresh eyes. But now she did, seeing Ellen's pleasure. And it was true. They were beautiful.

The little red-roofed farmhouse was very old, its chimney crooked and even the small, shuttered windows tilted at angles. A bird's nest, wispy with straw, was half hidden in the corner where the roof met the wall above a bedroom window. Nearby, a gnarled tree was still speckled with a few apples now long past ripe.

Mama and Kirsti had gone inside, but Annemarie and Ellen ran across the high-grassed meadow, through the late wildflowers. From nowhere, a gray kitten appeared and ran beside them, pouncing here and there upon imagined mice, pausing to lick its paws, and then darting off again. It pretended to ignore the girls, but looked back often to be certain they were still there, apparently pleased to have playmates.

The meadow ended at the sea, and the gray water licked there at damp brown grass flattened by the wind and bordered by smooth heavy stones.

"I have never been this close to the sea," Ellen said.

"Of course you have. You've been to the harbor in Copenhagen a million times."

Ellen laughed. "I mean the *real* sea, the way it is here. Open like this—a whole world of water."

Annemarie shook her head in amazement. To live in Denmark, a country surrounded by water, and never to have stood at its edge?

"Your parents are really city people, aren't they?"

Ellen nodded. "My mother is afraid of the ocean," she said, laughing. "She says it is too big for her. And too cold!"

The girls sat on a rock and took off their shoes and socks. They tiptoed across the damp stones and let the water touch their feet. It *was* cold. They giggled and stepped back.

Annemarie leaned down and picked up a brown leaf that floated back and forth with the movement of the water.

"Look," she said. "This leaf may have come from a tree in Sweden. It could have blown from a tree into the sea, and floated all the way across. See over there?" she said, pointing. "See the land? Way across there? That's Sweden."

Ellen cupped one hand over her eyes and looked across the water at the misty shoreline that was another country. "It's not so very far," she said.

"Maybe," Annemarie suggested, "standing over there are two girls just our age, looking across and saying, 'That's Denmark!'"

They squinted into the hazy distance, as if they might see Swedish children standing there and looking back. But it was too far. They saw only the hazy strip of land and two small boats bobbing up and down in the gray ruffles of separating water.

"I wonder if one of those is your Uncle Henrik's boat," Ellen said.

"Maybe. I can't tell. They're too far away. Uncle Henrik's boat is named the *Ingeborg*," she told Ellen, "for Mama."

Ellen looked around. "Does he keep it right here? Does he tie it up so that it won't float away?"

Annemarie laughed. "Oh, no. In town, at the harbor, there's a big dock, and all the fishing boats go and come from there. That's where they unload their fish. You should smell it! At night they are all there, anchored in the harbor."

"Annemarie! Ellen!" Mama's voice came across the meadow. The girls looked around, and saw her waving to them. They turned, picked up their shoes, and began walking toward the house. The kitten, who had settled comfortably on the stony shore, rose immediately and followed them.

"I took Ellen down to show her the sea," Annemarie explained when they reached the place where Mama waited. "She'd never been that close before! We started to wade, but it was too cold. I wish we had come in summer so we could swim."

"It's cold even then," Mama said. She looked around. "You didn't see anyone, did you? You didn't talk to anyone?"

Annemarie shook her head. "Just the kitten." Ellen had picked it up, and it lay purring in her arms as she stroked its small head and talked to it softly.

"I meant to warn you. You must stay away from people while we are here."

"But there's no one around here," Annemarie reminded her.

"Even so. If you see anyone at all—even someone you know, one of Henrik's friends—it is better if you come in the house. It is too difficult—maybe even dangerous—to explain who Ellen is."

Ellen looked up and bit her lip. "There aren't soldiers here, too?" she asked.

Mama sighed. "I'm afraid there are soldiers everywhere. And especially now. This is a bad time.

"Come in now and help me fix supper. Henrik will be home soon. Watch the step there; it's loose. Do you know what I have done? I found enough apples for applesauce. Even though there is no sugar, the apples are sweet. Henrik will bring home some fish and there is wood for the fire, so tonight we will be warm and well fed."

"It is not a bad time, then," Annemarie told her. "Not if there is applesauce."

Ellen kissed the kitten's head and let it leap from her arms to the ground. It darted away and disappeared in the tall grass. They followed Mama into the house.

That night, the girls dressed for bed in the small upstairs bedroom they were sharing, the same bedroom that had been Mama's when she was a little girl. Across the hall, Kirsti was already asleep in the wide bed that had once belonged to Annemarie's grandparents.

Ellen touched her neck after she had put on Annemarie's flower-sprigged nightgown, which Mama had packed.

"Where is my necklace?" she asked. "What did you do with it?"

"I hid it in a safe place," Annemarie told her. "A very secret place where no one will ever find it. And I will keep it there for you until it is safe for you to wear it again."

Ellen nodded. "Papa gave it to me when I was very small," she explained.

She sat down on the edge of the old bed and ran her fingers along the handmade quilt that covered it. The flowers and birds, faded now, had been stitched onto the quilt by Annemarie's great-grandmother many years before.

"I wish I knew where my parents are," Ellen said in a small voice as she outlined one of the appliquéd birds with her finger.

Annemarie didn't have an answer for her. She patted Ellen's hand and they sat together silently. Through the window, they could see a thin, round slice of moon appear through the clouds, against the pale sky. The Scandinavian night was not very dark yet, though soon, when winter came, the night would be not only dark but very long, night skies beginning in the late afternoon and lasting through morning.

From downstairs, they could hear Mama's voice, and Uncle Henrik's, talking, catching up on news. Mama missed her brother when she hadn't seen him for a while, Annemarie knew. They were very close. Mama always teased him gently for not marrying; she asked him, laughing, when they were together, whether he had found a good wife yet, one who would keep his house tidier. Henrik teased back, and told Mama that she should come to Gilleleje to live again so that he wouldn't have to do all the chores by himself.

For a moment, to Annemarie, listening, it seemed like all the earlier times, the happy visits to the farm in the past with summer daylight extending beyond bedtime, with the children tucked away in the bedrooms and the grownups downstairs talking.

But there was a difference. In the earlier times, she had always overheard laughter. Tonight there was no laughter at all.

Chapter 8 | There Has Been a Death

Tthrough a haze of dreams Annemarie heard Henrik rise and leave the house, headed for the barn with his milking pail, at daybreak. Later, when she woke again, it was morning. She could hear birds calling outside, one of them close by the window in the apple tree; and she could hear Mama below, in the kitchen, talking to Kirsti.

Ellen was still asleep. The night before, so shortened by the soldiers in the Copenhagen apartment, seemed long ago. Annemarie rose quietly so that she wouldn't wake her friend. She pulled on her clothes and went down the narrow, curved staircase to find her sister kneeling on the kitchen floor trying to make the gray kitten drink water from a bowl.

"Silly," she said. "Kittens like milk, not water."

"I am teaching this one new habits," Kirsti explained importantly. "And I have named him Thor, for the God of Thunder."

Annemarie burst out laughing. She looked at the tiny kitten, who was shaking his head, irritated at his wet whiskers as Kirsti kept trying to dip his face to the water. "God of Thunder?" Annemarie said. "He looks as if he would run and *hide* if there were a thunderstorm!"

"He has a mother someplace who would comfort him, I imagine," Mama said. "And when he wants milk, he'll find his mama."

"Or he could go visit the cow," Kirsti said.

Although Uncle Henrik no longer raised crops on the farm, as his parents had, he still kept a cow, who munched happily on the meadow grass and gave a little milk each day in return. Now and then he was able to send cheese into Copenhagen to his sister's family. This morning, Annemarie noticed with delight, Mama had made oatmeal, and there was a pitcher of cream on the table. It was a very long time since she had tasted cream. At home they had bread and tea every morning.

Mama followed Annemarie's eyes to the pitcher. "Fresh from Blossom," she said. "Henrik milks her every morning before he leaves for the boat.

"And," she added, "there's butter, too. Usually not even Henrik has butter, but he managed to save a little this time."

"Save a little from what?" Annemarie asked, spooning oatmeal into a flowered bowl. "Don't tell me the soldiers try to—what's the word?—*relocate* butter, too?" She laughed at her own joke.

But it wasn't a joke at all, though Mama laughed ruefully. "They do," she said. "They relocate all the farmers' butter, right into the stomach of their army! I suppose that if they knew Henrik had kept this tiny bit, they would come with guns and march it away, down the path!"

Kirsti joined their laughter, as the three of them pictured a mound of frightened butter under military arrest. The kitten darted away when Kirsti's attention was distracted, and settled on the windowsill. Suddenly, here in this sunlit kitchen, with cream in a pitcher and a bird in the apple tree beside the door—and out in the Kattegat, where Uncle Henrik, surrounded by bright blue sky and water, pulled in his nets filled with shiny silver fish—suddenly the specter of guns and grim-faced soldiers seemed nothing more than a ghost story, a joke with which to frighten children in the dark.

Ellen appeared in the kitchen doorway, smiling sleepily, and Mama put another flowered bowl of steaming oatmeal on the old wooden table.

"*Cream*," Annemarie said, gesturing to the pitcher with a grin.

All day long the girls played out of doors under the brilliant clear sky and sun. Annemarie took Ellen to the small pasture beyond the barn and introduced her to Blossom, who gave a lazy, rough-textured lick to the palm of Ellen's hand when she extended it timidly. The kitten scampered about and chased flying insects across the meadow. The girls picked armfuls of wildflowers dried brown, now, by the early fall chill, and arranged them in pots and pitchers until the table tops were crowded with their bouquets.

Inside the house, Mama scrubbed and dusted, tsk-tsking at Uncle Henrik's untidy housekeeping. She took the rugs out to the clothesline and beat them with a stick, scattering dust into the air.

"He needs a wife," she said, shaking her head, and attacked the old wooden floors with a broom while the rugs aired.

"Just look at this," she said, opening the door to the little-used formal living room with its old-fashioned furniture. "He *never* dusts." And she picked up her cleaning rags.

"And, Kirsti," she added, "the God of Thunder made a very small rain shower in the corner of the kitchen floor. Keep an eye on him."

Late in the afternoon, Uncle Henrik came home. He grinned when he saw the newly cleaned and polished house, the double doors to the living room wide open, the rugs aired, and the windows washed.

"Henrik, you need a wife," Mama scolded him.

Uncle Henrik laughed and joined Mama on the steps near the kitchen door. "Why do I need a wife, when I have a sister?" he asked in his booming voice.

Mama sighed, but her eyes were twinkling. "And you need to stay home more often to take care of the house. This step is broken, and there is a leaking faucet in the kitchen. And —"

Henrik was grinning at her, shaking his head in mock dismay. "And there are mice in the attic, and my brown sweater has a big moth hole in the sleeve, and if I don't wash the windows soon—"

They laughed together.

"Anyway," Mama said, "I have opened every window, Henrik, to let the air in, and the sunlight. Thank goodness it is such a beautiful day."

"Tomorrow will be a day for fishing," Henrik said, his smile disappearing.

Annemarie, listening, recognized the odd phrase. Papa had said something like it on the telephone. "Is the weather good for fishing, Henrik?" Papa had asked. But what did it mean? Henrik went fishing every day, rain or shine. Denmark's fishermen didn't wait for sunny days to take their boats out and throw their nets into the sea. Annemarie, silent, sitting with Ellen under the apple tree, watched her uncle.

Mama looked at him. "The weather is right?" she asked.

Henrik nodded and looked at the sky. He smelled the air. "I will be going back to the boat tonight after supper. We will leave very early in the morning. I will stay on the boat all night."

Annemarie wondered what it would be like to be on a boat all night. To lie at anchor, hearing the sea slap against the side. To see the stars from your place on the sea.

"You have prepared the living room?" Uncle Henrik asked suddenly.

Mama nodded. "It is cleaned, and I moved the furniture a bit to make room.

"And you saw the flowers," she added. "I hadn't thought of it, but the girls picked dried flowers from the meadow."

"Prepared the living room for what?" Annemarie asked. "Why did you move the furniture?"

Mama looked at Uncle Henrik. He had reached down for the kitten, scampering past, and now held it against his chest and scratched its chin gently. It arched its small back with pleasure.

"Well, girls," he said, "it is a sad event, but not *too* sad, really, because she was very, very old. There has been a death, and tonight your Great-aunt Birte will be resting in the living room, in her casket, before she is buried tomorrow. It is the old custom, you know, for the dead to rest at home, and their loved ones to be with them before burial."

Kirsti was listening with a fascinated look. "Right here?" she asked. "A dead person right here?"

Annemarie said nothing. She was confused. This was the first she had heard of a death in the family. No one had called Copenhagen to say that there had been a death. No one had seemed sad.

And—most puzzling of all—she had never heard the name before. Great-aunt Birte. *Surely* she would have known if she had a relative by that name. Kirsti might not; Kirsti was little and didn't pay attention to such things.

But Annemarie did. She had always been fascinated by her mother's stories of her own childhood. She remembered the names of all the cousins, the great-aunts, and -uncles: who had been a tease, who had been a grouch, who had been such a scold that her husband had finally moved away to a different house, though they continued to have dinner together every night. Such wonderful, interesting stories, filled with the colorful personalities of her mother's family.

And Annemarie was quite, quite certain, though she said nothing. There was no Great-aunt Birte. She didn't exist.

Chapter 9 | Why Are You Lying?

Annemarie went outside alone after supper. Through the open kitchen window she could hear Mama and Ellen talking as they washed the dishes. Kirsti, she knew, was busy on the floor, playing with the old dolls she had found upstairs, the dolls that had been Mama's once, long ago. The kitten had fled when she tried to dress it, and disappeared.

She wandered to the barn, where Uncle Henrik was milking Blossom. He was kneeling on the straw-covered floor beside the cow, his shoulder pressed against her heavy side, his strong tanned hands rhythmically urging her milk into the spotless bucket. The God of Thunder sat alertly poised nearby, watching.

Blossom looked up at Annemarie with big brown eyes, and moved her wrinkled mouth like an old woman adjusting false teeth.

Annemarie leaned against the ancient splintery wood of the barn wall and listened to the sharp rattling sound of the streams of milk as they hit the sides of the bucket. Uncle Henrik glanced over at her and smiled without pausing in the rhythm of milking. He didn't say anything.

Through the barn windows, the pinkish light of sunset fell in irregular shapes upon the stacked hay. Flecks of dust and straw floated there, in the light.

"Uncle Henrik," Annemarie said suddenly, her voice cold, "you are lying to me. You and Mama both."

His strong hands continued, deftly pressing like a pulse against the cow. The steady streams of milk still came. He looked at her again, his deep blue eyes kind and questioning. "You are angry," he said.

"Yes. Mama has never lied to me before. Never. But I know there is no Great-aunt Birte. Never once, in all the stories I've heard, in all the old pictures I've seen, has there been a Great-aunt Birte."

Uncle Henrik sighed. Blossom looked back at him, as if to say "Almost done," and, indeed, the streams of milk lessened and slowed.

He tugged at the cow gently but firmly, pulling down the last of the milk. The bucket was half full, frothy on the top. Finally he set it aside and washed the cow's udder with a clean damp cloth. Then he lifted the bucket to a shelf and covered it. He rubbed the cow's neck affectionately. At last he turned to Annemarie as he wiped his own hands with the cloth.

"How brave are you, little Annemarie?" he asked suddenly.

She was startled. And dismayed. It was a question she did not want to be asked. When she asked it of herself, she didn't like her own answer.

"Not very," she confessed, looking at the floor of the barn.

Tall Uncle Henrik knelt before her so that his face was level with hers. Behind him, Blossom lowered her head, grasped a mouthful of hay in her mouth, and drew it in with her tongue. The kitten cocked its head, waiting, still hoping for spilled milk.

"I think that is not true," Uncle Henrik said. "I think you are like your mama, and like your papa, and like me. Frightened, but determined, and if the time came to be brave, I am quite sure you would be very, very brave.

"But," he added, "it is much *easier* to be brave if you do not know everything. And so your mama does not know everything. Neither do I. We know only what we need to know.

"Do you understand what I am saying?" he asked, looking into her eyes.

Annemarie frowned. She wasn't sure. What did bravery mean? She had been very frightened the day—not long ago, though now it seemed far in the past—when the soldier had stopped her on the street and asked questions in his rough voice.

And she had not known everything then. She had not known that the Germans were going to take away the Jews. And so, when the soldier asked, looking at Ellen that day, "What is your friend's name?" she had been able to answer him, even though she was frightened. If she had known everything, it would not have been as easy to be brave.

She began to understand, just a little. "Yes," she said to Uncle Henrik, "I think I understand."

"You guessed correctly," he told her. "There is no Great-aunt Birte, and never has been. Your mama lied to you and so did I.

"We did so," he explained "to help you to be brave, because we love you. Will you forgive us for that?"

Annemarie nodded. She felt older, suddenly.

"And I am not going to tell you any more, not now, for the same reason. Do you understand?"

Annemarie nodded again. Suddenly there was a noise outside. Uncle Henrik's shoulders stiffened. He rose quickly, went to the window of the barn, stood in the shadows, and looked out. Then he turned back to Annemarie.

"It is the hearse," he said. "It is Great-aunt Birte, who never was." He smiled wryly. "So, my little friend, it is time for the night of mourning to begin. Are you ready?"

Annemarie took her uncle's hand and he led her from the barn.

*

The gleaming wooden casket rested on supports in the center of the living room and was surrounded by the fragile, papery flowers that Annemarie and Ellen had picked that afternoon. Lighted candles stood in holders on the table and cast a soft, flickering light. The hearse had gone, and the solemn-faced men who had carried the casket indoors had gone with it, after speaking quietly to Uncle Henrik.

Kirsti had gone to bed reluctantly, complaining that she wanted to stay up with the others, that she was grownup enough, that she had never before seen a dead person in a closed-up box, that it wasn't *fair*. But Mama had been firm, and finally Kirsti, sulking, had trudged upstairs with her dolls under one arm and the kitten under the other.

Ellen was silent, and had a sad expression. "I'm so sorry your Aunt Birte died," Annemarie heard her say to Mama, who smiled sadly and thanked her.

Annemarie had listened and said nothing. So now I, too, am lying, she thought, and to my very best friend. I could tell Ellen that it isn't true, that there is no Great-aunt Birte. I could take her aside and whisper the secret to her so that she wouldn't have to feel sad.

But she didn't. She understood that she was protecting Ellen the way her mother had protected her. Although she didn't understand what was happening, or why the casket was there—or who, in truth, was in it—she knew that it was better, safer, for Ellen to believe in Great-aunt Birte. So she said nothing.

Other people came as the night sky grew darker. A man and a woman, both of them dressed in dark clothing, the woman carrying a sleeping baby, appeared at the door, and Uncle Henrik gestured them inside. They nodded to Mama and to the girls. They went, following Uncle Henrik, to the living room and sat down quietly.

"Friends of Great-aunt Birte," Mama said quietly in response to Annemarie's questioning look. Annemarie knew that Mama was lying again, and she could see that Mama understood that she knew. They looked at each other for a long time and said nothing. In that moment, with that look, they became equals.

From the living room came the sound of a sleepy baby's brief wail. Annemarie glanced through the door and saw the woman open her blouse and begin to nurse the infant, who quieted.

Another man arrived: an old man, bearded. Quietly he went to the living room and sat down, saying nothing to the others, who only glanced at him. The young woman lifted her baby's blanket, covering its face and her own breast. The old man bent his head forward and closed his eyes, as if he were praying. His mouth moved silently, forming words that no one could hear.

Annemarie stood in the doorway, watching the mourners as they sat in the candlelit room. Then she turned back to the kitchen and began to help Ellen and Mama as they prepared food.

In Copenhagen, she remembered, when Lise died, friends had come to their apartment every evening. All of them had brought food so that Mama wouldn't need to cook.

Why hadn't these people brought food? Why didn't they talk? In Copenhagen, even though the talk was sad, people had spoken softly to one another and to Mama and Papa. They had talked about Lise, remembering happier times.

Thinking about it as she sliced cheese in the kitchen, Annemarie realized that these people had nothing to talk about. They couldn't speak of happier times with Great-aunt Birte when there had never been a Great-aunt Birte at all.

Uncle Hernik came into the kitchen. He glanced at his watch and then at Mama. "It's getting late," he said. "I should go to the boat." He looked worried. He blew out the candles so that there would be no light at all, and opened the door. He stared beyond the gnarled apple tree into the darkness.

"Good. Here they come," he said in a low, relieved voice. "Ellen, come with me."

Ellen looked questioningly toward Mama, who nodded. "Go with Henrik," she said.

Annemarie watched, still holding the wedge of firm cheese in her hand, as Ellen followed Uncle Henrik into the yard. She could hear a sharp, low cry from Ellen, and then the sound of voices speaking softly.

In a moment Uncle Henrik returned. Behind him was Peter Neilsen.

Tonight Peter went first to Mama and hugged her. Then he hugged Annemarie and kissed her on the cheek. But he said nothing. There was no playfulness to his affection tonight, just a sense of urgency, of worry. He went immediately to the living room, looked around, and nodded to the silent people there.

Ellen was still outside. But in a moment the door opened and she returned—held tightly, like a little girl, her bare legs dangling, against her father's chest. Her mother was beside them.

Chapter 10 | Let Us Open the Casket

YOU ARE ALL HERE NOW," Uncle Henrik said, looking around the living room. "I must go."

Annemarie stood in the wide doorway, looking in from the hall. The baby slept now, and its mother looked tired. Her husband sat beside her, his arm across her shoulders. The old man's head was still bent.

Peter sat alone, leaning forward with his elbows on his knees. It was clear that he was deep in thought.

On the sofa Ellen sat between her parents, one hand clasped tightly in her mother's. She looked up at Annemarie but didn't smile. Annemarie felt a surge of sadness; the bond of their friendship had not broken, but it was as if Ellen had moved now into a different world, the world of her own family and whatever lay ahead for them.

The elderly bearded man looked up suddenly as Uncle Henrik prepared to go. "God keep you safe," he said in a firm but quiet voice.

Henrik nodded. "God keep us all safe," he replied. Then he turned and left the room. A moment later Annemarie heard him leave the house.

Mama brought the teapot from the kitchen, and a tray of cups. Annemarie helped her pass the cups around. No one spoke.

"Annemarie," Mama whispered to her in the hall, "You may go to bed if you want to. It is very late."

Annemarie shook her head. But she was tired. She could see that Ellen was, too; her friend's head was leaning on her mother's shoulder, and her eyes closed now and then.

Finally Annemarie went to the empty rocking chair in the corner of the living room and curled there with her head against its soft, padded back. She dozed.

She was startled from her half sleep by the sudden sweep of headlights, through the sheer curtains and across the room, as a car pulled up outside. The car doors slammed. Everyone in the room tensed, but no one spoke.

She heard—as if in a recurring nightmare—the pounding on the door, and then the heavy, frighteningly familiar staccato of boots on the kitchen floor. The woman with the baby gasped and began, suddenly, to weep.

The male, accented voice from the kitchen was loud. "We have observed," he said, "that an unusual number of people have gathered at this house tonight. What is the explanation?"

"There has been a death," Mama's voice replied calmly. "It is always our custom to gather and pay our respects when a family member dies. I am sure you are familiar with our customs."

One of the officers pushed Mama ahead of him from the kitchen and entered the living room. There were others behind him. They filled the wide doorway. As always, their boots gleamed. Their guns. Their helmets. All of them gleamed in the candlelight.

Annemarie watched as the man's eyes moved around the room. He looked for a long time at the casket. Then he moved his gaze, focusing on each person in turn. When his eyes reached her, she looked back at him steadily.

"Who died?" he asked harshly.

No one answered. They watched Annemarie, and she realized that the officer was directing the question at her.

Now she knew for certain what Uncle Henrik had meant when he had talked to her in the barn. To be brave came more easily if you knew nothing.

She swallowed. "My Great-aunt Birte," she lied, in a firm voice.

The officer moved forward suddenly, across the room, to the casket. He placed one gloved hand on its lid. "Poor Great-aunt Birte," he said, in a condescending voice.

"I *do* know your customs," he said, turning his gaze toward Mama, who still stood in the doorway. "And I know it is the custom to pay one's respects by looking your loved one in the face. It seems odd to me that you have closed this coffin up so tightly." His hand was in a fist, and he rubbed it across the edge of the polished lid.

"Why is it not open?" he demanded. "Let us open it up and take one last look at Great-aunt Birte!"

Annemarie saw Peter, across the room, stiffen in his chair, lift his chin, and reach slowly with one hand toward his side.

Mama walked quickly across the room, directly to the casket, directly to the officer. "You're right," she said. "The doctor said it should be closed, because Aunt Birte died of typhus, and he said that there was a chance the germs would still be there, would still be dangerous. But what does he know—only a country doctor, and an old man at that? Surely typhus germs wouldn't linger in a dead person! And dear Aunt Birte; I have been longing to see her face, to kiss her goodbye. Of *course* we will open the casket! I am glad you suggested—"

With a swift motion the Nazi officer slapped Mama across her face. She staggered backward, and a white mark on her cheek darkened.

"You foolish woman," he spat. "To think that we have any interest in seeing the body of your diseased aunt! Open it after we leave," he said.

With one gloved thumb he pressed a candle flame into darkness. The hot wax spattered the table. "Put all these candles out," he said, "or pull the curtains."

Then he strode to the doorway and left the room. Motionless, silent, one hand to her cheek, Mama listened—they all listened—as the uniformed men left the house. In a moment they heard the car doors, the sound of its engine, and finally they heard it drive away.

"Mama!" Annemarie cried.

Her mother shook her head quickly, and glanced at the open window covered only by the sheer curtain. Annemarie understood. There might still be soldiers outside, watching, listening.

Peter stood and drew the dark curtains across the windows. He relit the extinguished candle. Then he reached for the old Bible that had always been there, on the mantel. He opened it quickly and said "I will read a psalm."

His eyes turned to the page he had opened at random, and he began to read in a strong voice.

O praise the Lord.
How good it is to sing psalms to our God!
How pleasant to praise him!
The Lord is rebuilding Jerusalem;
He gathers in the scattered sons of Israel.
It is he who heals the broken in spirit
And binds up their wounds,

He who numbers the stars one by one . . .

Mama sat down and listened. Gradually they each began to relax. Annemarie could see the old man across the room, moving his lips as Peter read; he knew the ancient psalm by heart.

Annemarie didn't. The words were unfamiliar to her, and she tried to listen, tried to understand, tried to forget the war and the Nazis, tried not to cry, tried to be brave. The night breeze moved the dark curtains at the open windows. Outside, she knew, the sky was speckled with stars. How could anyone number them one by one, as the psalm said? There were too many. The sky was too big.

Ellen had said that her mother was frightened of the ocean, that it was too cold, too big.

The sky was, too, thought Annemarie. The whole *world* was: too cold, too big. And too cruel.

Peter read on, in his firm voice, though it was clear he was tired. The long minutes passed. They seemed hours.

Finally, still reading, he moved quietly to the window. He closed the Bible and listened to the quiet night. Then he looked around the room.

"Now," he said, "it is time."

First he closed the windows. Then he went to the casket and opened the lid.

Chapter 11 | Will We See You Again Soon, Peter?

ANNEMARIE BLINKED. Across the dark room, she saw Ellen, too, peering into the narrow wooden box in surprise.

There was no one in the casket at all. Instead, it seemed to be stuffed with folded blankets and articles of clothing.

Peter began to lift the things out and distribute them to the old man with the beard.

"It will be very cold," he murmured. "Put them on." He found a thick sweater for Mrs. Rosen, and a woolen jacket for Ellen's father. After a moment of rummaging through the folded things, he found a smaller winter jacket, and handed it to Ellen.

Annemarie watched as Ellen took the jacket in her arms and looked at it. It was patched and worn. It was true that there had been few new clothes for anyone during the recent years; but still, Ellen's mother had always managed to make clothes for her daughter, often using old things that she was able to take apart and refashion in a way that made them seem brand-new. Never had Ellen worn anything so shabby and old.

But she put it on, pulled it around her, and buttoned the mismatched buttons.

Peter, his arms full of the odd pieces of clothing, looked toward the silent couple with the infant. "I'm sorry," he said to them. "There is nothing for a baby."

"I'll find something," Mama said quickly. "The baby must be warm." She left the room and was back in a moment with Kirsti's thick red sweater.

"Here," she said softly to the mother. "It will be much too big, but that will make it even warmer for him."

The woman spoke for the first time. "Her," she whispered. "She's a girl. Her name is Rachel."

Mama smiled and helped her direct the sleeping baby's arms into the sleeves of the sweater. Together they buttoned the heart-shaped buttons—how Kirsti loved that sweater, with its heart buttons!—until the tiny child was completely encased in the warm red wool. Her eyelids fluttered but she didn't wake.

Peter reached into his pocket and took something out. He went to the parents and leaned down toward the baby. He opened the lid of the small bottle in his hand.

"How much does she weigh?" Peter asked.

"She was seven pounds when she was born," the young woman replied. "She's gained a little, but not very much. Maybe she weighs eight pounds now, no more."

"A few drops will be enough, then. It has no taste. She won't even notice."

The mother tightened her arms around the baby and looked up at Peter, pleading. "Please, no," she said. "She always sleeps all night. Please, she doesn't need it, I promise. She won't cry."

Peter's voice was firm. "We can't take a chance," he said. He inserted the dropper of the bottle into the baby's tiny mouth, and squeezed a few drops of liquid onto her tongue. The baby yawned, and swallowed. The mother closed her eyes; her husband gripped her shoulder.

Next, Peter removed the folded blankets from the coffin, one by one, and handed them around. "Carry these with you," he said. "You will need them later, for warmth."

Annemarie's mother moved around the room and gave each person a small package of food: the cheese and bread and apples that Annemarie had helped her prepare in the kitchen hours before.

Finally, Peter took a paper-wrapped packet from the inside of his own jacket. He looked around the room, at the assembled people now dressed in the bulky winter clothing, and then motioned to Mr. Rosen, who followed him to the hall.

Annemarie could overhear their conversation. "Mr. Rosen," Peter said, "I must get this to Henrik. But I might not see him. I am going to take the others only to the harbor and they will go to the boat alone.

"I want you to deliver this. Without fail. It is of great importance." There was a moment of silence in the hall, and Annemarie knew that Peter must be giving the packet to Mr. Rosen.

Annemarie could see it protruding from Mr. Rosen's pocket when he returned to the room and sat down again. She could see, too, that Mr. Rosen had a puzzled look. He didn't know what the packet contained. He hadn't asked.

It was one more time, Annemarie realized, when they protected one another by not telling. If Mr. Rosen knew, he might be frightened. If Mr. Rosen knew, he might be in danger.

So he hadn't asked. And Peter hadn't explained.

"Now," Peter said, looking at his watch, "I will lead the first group. You, and you, and you." He gestured to the old man and to the young people with their baby.

"Inge," he said. Annemarie realized that it was the first time that she had heard Peter Neilsen call her mother by her first name; before, it had always been "Mrs. Johansen"; or, in the old days, during the merriment and excitement of his engagement to Lise, it had been, occasionally, "Mama." Now it was Inge. It was as if he had moved beyond his own youth and had taken his place in the world of adults. Her mother nodded and waited for his instructions.

"You wait twenty minutes, and then bring the Rosens. Don't come sooner. We must be separate on the path so there is less chance of being seen."

Mrs. Johansen nodded again.

"Come directly back to the house after you have seen the Rosens safely to Henrik. Stay in the shadows and on the back path—you know that, of course.

"By the time you get the Rosens to the boat," Peter went on, "I will be gone. As soon as I deliver my group, I must move on. There is other work to be done tonight."

He turned to Annemarie. "So I will say goodbye to you now."

Annemarie went to him and gave him a hug. "But we will see you again soon?" she asked.

"I hope so," Peter said. "Very soon. Don't grow much more, or you will be taller than I am, little Longlegs!"

Annemarie smiled, but Peter's comment was no longer the lighthearted fun of the past. It was only a brief grasp at something that had gone.

Peter kissed Mama wordlessly. Then he wished the Rosens Godspeed, and he led the others through the door.

Mama, Annemarie, and the Rosens sat in silence. There was a slight commotion outside the door, and Mama went quickly to look out. In a moment she was back.

"It's all right," she said, in response to their looks. "The old man stumbled. But Peter helped him up. He didn't seem to be hurt. Maybe just his pride," she added, smiling a bit.

It was an odd word: *pride*. Annemarie looked at the Rosens, sitting there, wearing the misshapen, ill-fitting clothing, holding ragged blankets folded in their arms, their faces drawn and tired. She remembered the earlier, happier times: Mrs. Rosen, her hair neatly combed and covered, lighting the Sabbath candles, saying the ancient prayer. And Mr. Rosen, sitting in the big chair in their living room, studying his thick books, correcting papers, adjusting his glasses, looking up now and then to complain good-naturedly about the lack of decent light. She remembered Ellen in the school play, moving confidently across the stage, her gestures sure, her voice clear.

All of those things, those sources of pride—the candlesticks, the books, the daydreams of theater—had been left behind in Copenhagen. They had nothing with them now; there was only the clothing of unknown people for warmth, the food from Henrik's farm for survival, and the dark path ahead, through the woods, to freedom.

Annemarie realized, though she had not really been told, that Uncle Henrik was going to take them, in his boat, across the sea to Sweden. She knew how frightened Mrs. Rosen was of the sea: its width, its depth, its cold. She knew how frightened Ellen was of the soldiers, with their guns and boots, who were certainly looking for them. And she knew how frightened they all must be of the future.

But their shoulders were as straight as they had been in the past: in the classroom, on the stage, at the Sabbath table. So there were other sources, too, of pride, and they had not left everything behind.

Chapter 12 | Where Was Mama?

MR. ROSEN TRIPPED on the loose step outside the kitchen door. His wife grasped his arm, and he regained his balance.

"It's very dark," Mama whispered as they stood in the yard with their blankets and bundles of food gathered in their arms, "and we can't use any kind of light. I'll go first—I know the way very well—and you follow me. Try not to stumble over the tree roots in the path. Feel carefully with your feet. The path is uneven.

"And be very, very quiet," she added unnecessarily.

The night was quiet, too. A slight breeze moved in the tops of the trees, and from across the meadow came the sound of the sea's movement, which was a constant sound here and had always been. But no birds called or cried here now, in the night. The cow slept silently in the barn, the kitten upstairs in Kirsti's arms.

There were stars here and there, dotting the sky among thin clouds, but no moon. Annemarie shivered, standing at the foot of the steps.

"Come," Mama murmured, and she moved away from the house.

One by one the Rosens turned and hugged Annemarie silently. Ellen came to her last; the two girls held each other.

"I'll come back someday," Ellen whispered fiercely. "I *promise*."

"I know you will," Annemarie whispered back, holding her friend tightly.

Then they were gone, Mama and the Rosens. Annemarie was alone. She went into the house, crying suddenly, and closed the door against the night.

The lid of the casket was closed again. Now the room was empty; there was no sign of the people who had sat there for those hours. Annemarie wiped her eyes with the back of her hand. She opened the dark curtains and the windows; she curled once more in the rocker, trying to relax; she traced their route in her mind. She knew the old path, too—not as well as her mother, who had followed it almost every day of her childhood with her dog scampering behind. But Annemarie had often walked to town and back that way, and she remembered the turns, the twisted trees whose gnarled roots pushed the earth now and then into knotted clumps, and the thick bushes that often flowered in early summer.

She walked with them in her mind, feeling the way through the darkness. It would take them, she thought, half an hour to reach the place where Uncle Henrik was waiting with his boat. Mama would leave them there—pausing a minute, no more, for a final hug—and then she would turn and come home. It would be faster for Mama alone, with no need to wait as the Rosens, unfamiliar with the path, slowly felt their way along. Mama would hurry, sure-footed now, back to her children.

The clock in the hall struck once; it was two-thirty in the morning. Her mother would be home in an hour, Annemarie decided. She rocked gently back and forth in the old chair. Mama would be home by three-thirty.

She thought of Papa, back in Copenhagen alone. He would be awake, too. He would be wishing he could have come, but knowing, too, that he must come and go as always: to the corner store for the newspaper, to his office when morning came. Now he would be afraid for them, and watching the clock, waiting for word that the Rosens were safe, that Mama and the girls were here at the farm, starting a new day with the sun shining through the kitchen window and cream on their oatmeal.

It was harder for the ones who were waiting, Annemarie knew. Less danger, perhaps, but more fear.

She yawned, and her head nodded. She fell asleep, and it was a sleep as thin as the night clouds, dotted with dreams that came and went like the stars.

Light woke her. But it was not really morning, not yet. It was only the first hint of a slightly lightening sky: a pale gleam at the edge of the meadow, a sign that far away somewhere, to the east where Sweden still slept, morning would be coming soon. Dawn would creep across the Swedish farmland and coast; then it would wash little Denmark with light and move across the North Sea to wake Norway.

Annemarie blinked in confusion, sitting up, remembering after a moment where she was and why. But it was not right, the pale light at the horizon—it should be dark still. It should still be night.

She stood stiffly, stretching her legs, and went to the hall to look at the old clock. It was past four o'clock.

Where was Mama?

Perhaps she had come home, not wanted to wake Annemarie, and had gone to bed herself. Surely that was it. Mama must have been exhausted; she had been up all night, had made the dangerous journey to the boat, and returned through the dark woods, wanting only to sleep.

Quickly Annemarie went up the narrow staircase. The door to the bedroom where she had slept with Ellen was open. The two small beds were neatly made covered with the old quilts, and empty.

Beside it, Uncle Henrik's door was open, too; and his bed, too, was unused and empty. Despite her worry, Annemarie smiled slightly when she saw some of Henrik's clothes crumpled in a chair and a pair of shoes, caked with the barnyard dirt, lying on the floor.

He needs a wife, she said to herself, imitating Mama.

The door to the other bedroom, the one Kirsti and Mama were sharing, was closed. Quietly, not wanting to wake them, Annemarie pushed it open.

The kitten's ear moved, standing up straight; its eyes opened wide, and it raised its head and yawned. It pried itself out of Kirsti's arms, stretched, and then jumped lightly to the floor and came to Annemarie. It rubbed itself against her leg and purred.

Kirsti sighed and turned in her sleep; one arm, free now of the kitten's warmth and comfort, flung itself across the pillow.

There was no one else in the wide bed.

Annemarie moved quickly to the window, which overlooked the clearing that led to the path's entrance. The light outside was still dim, and she peered through the dimness, trying to see, looking for the opening in the trees where the path began, looking for Mama hurrying home.

After a second she saw a shape there: something unfamiliar, something that had not been there the day before. A dark shape, no more than a blurred heap, at the beginning of the path. Annemarie squinted, forcing her eyes to understand, needing to understand, and not wanting to understand.

The shape moved. And she knew. It was her mother, lying on the earth.

Chapter 13 | Run! As Fast As You Can!

STILL MOVING QUIETLY so as not to wake her sister, Annemarie sped down the stairs and through the kitchen door. Her foot caught the loose step and she faltered for a moment, righting herself, then dashed across the ground to the place where her mother lay.

"Mama!" she called desperately. "Mama!"

"Shhh," Mama said, raising her head. "I'm all right!"

"But, Mama," Annemarie asked, kneeling beside her, "what's wrong? What happened?"

Her mother pulled herself to a sitting position. She winced in pain. "I'm all right, really. Don't worry. And the Rosens are with Henrik. That's the important thing."

She smiled a little, though her face was drawn with pain and she bit her lip, the smile fading. "We got there quite quickly, even though it was still so dark and it was difficult for the Rosens, not knowing the path. Henrik was there waiting, on the boat, and he took them aboard and down below so quickly to the cabin that they were invisible in an instant. He said the others were already there; Peter got them there safely, too.

"So I turned and hurried home. I was so anxious to get back to you girls. I should have been more careful." Talking softly, she brushed some grass and dirt from her hands.

"Can you believe it? I was very nearly here—well, maybe just halfway—when I tripped over a root and went sprawling."

Mama sighed. "So clumsy," she said, as if she were scolding herself. "I'm afraid my ankle is broken, Annemarie. Thank goodness it is nothing worse. An ankle mends. And I am home, and the Rosens are with Henrik.

"You should have seen me, Annemarie," she said, shaking her head with a wry look. "Your proper mama, crawling inch by inch! I probably looked like a drunkard!"

She reached for Annemarie's arm. "Here, let me lean on you. I think if you support me on this side, I can make my way up to the house. Goodness, what a clumsy fool I am! Here, let me put my arm over your shoulders. You're such a good, strong, brave girl. Now—very slowly. There."

Mama's face was white with pain. Annemarie could see it even through the faint light of the approaching dawn. She hobbled, leaning heavily on her daughter, pausing again and again, toward the house.

"When we get inside, I'll have a cup of tea and then we'll call the doctor. I'll tell him that I fell on the stairs. You'll have to help me wash away the grass and twigs. Here, Annemarie, let me rest for a minute."

They had reached the house, and Mama sank down to the steps and sat. She took several deep breaths.

Annemarie sat beside her and held her hand. "Mama, I was so worried when you didn't come back."

Mama nodded. "I knew you would be. I thought of you, worrying, as I dragged myself along. But here I am—safe with you, now. Everything is fine. What time is it"

"It must be four-thirty, or close to it."

"They will sail soon." Mama turned her head and gazed across the meadow to the sea and the vast sky above it. There were no stars now, only the gray, pale sky, with pinkness at its border. "Soon they will be safe, too."

Annemarie relaxed. She stroked her mother's hand and looked down at the discolored, swollen ankle.

"Mama, what is this?" she asked suddenly, reaching into the grass at the foot of the steps.

Mama looked. She gasped. "Oh, my God," she said.

Annemarie picked it up. She recognized it now, knew what it was. It was the packet that Peter had given to Mr. Rosen.

"Mr. Rosen tripped on the step, remember? It must have fallen from his pocket. We'll have to save it and give it back to Peter." Annemarie handed it to her mother. "Do you know what it is?"

Her mother didn't answer. Her face was stricken. She looked at the path and down at her ankle.

"It's important, isn't it, Mama? It was for Uncle Henrik. I remember Peter said it was very important. I heard him tell Mr. Rosen."

Her mother tried to stand, but fell back against the steps with a groan. "My God," she murmured again. "It may all have been for nothing."

Annemarie took the packet from her mother's hand and stood. "I will take it," she said. "I know the way, and it's almost light now. I can run like the wind."

Mama spoke quickly, her voice tense. "Annemarie, go into the house and get the small basket on the table. Quickly, quickly. Put an apple into it, and some cheese. Put this pack underneath; do you understand? *Hurry.*"

Annemarie did instantly as she was told. The basket. The packet, at the bottom. She covered it with a napkin. Then some wrapped cheese. An apple. She glanced around the kitchen, saw some bread, and added that. The little basket was full. She took it to where her mother was.

"You must run to the boat. If anyone should stop you —"

"Who would stop me?"

"Annemarie, you understand how dangerous this is. If any soldiers see you, if they stop you, you must pretend to be nothing more than a little girl. A silly, empty-headed little girl, taking lunch to a fisherman, a foolish uncle who forgot his bread and cheese."

"Mama, what *is* it in the bottom?"

But her mother still didn't answer the question. "Go," she said firmly. "Go right now. And *run!* As fast as you can!"

Annemarie kissed her mother quickly, grabbed the basket from her mother's lap, turned, and ran toward the path.

| Chapter 14 | # On the Dark Path |

ONLY NOW, ENTERING THE WOODS on the foot path, did Annemarie realize how cold the dawn was. She had watched and helped, earlier, as the others donned sweaters, jackets, and coats; and she had peered into the night, following them with her eyes, as they moved silently off, bulky in their garments, blankets in their arms.

But she wore only a light sweater over her cotton dress. Though the October day, later, would be warmed by sunlight, now it was gray, chilly, and damp. She shivered.

The path curved, and she could no longer look behind her and see the clearing with the farmhouse outlined against the pale sky and the lightening meadow beyond. Now there were only the dark woods ahead; underfoot, the path, latticed with thick roots hidden under the fallen leaves, was invisible. She felt her way with her feet, trying not to stumble.

The handle of the straw basket scratched her arm through her sweater. She shifted it and tried to run.

She thought of a story she had often told to Kirsti as they cuddled in bed at night.

"Once upon a time there was a little girl," she told herself silently, "who had a beautiful red cloak. Her mother had made it for her.

"She wore it so often that everyone called her Little Red Riding-Hood."

Kirsti would always interrupt there. "Why was it called a red riding hood?" Kirsti would ask. "Why didn't they just call her Little Red-Cloak?"

"Well, it had a hood that covered her head. She had beautiful curls, like you, Kirsti. Maybe someday Mama will make you a coat with a hood to cover your curls and keep you warm."

"But why," Kirsti would ask, "was it a *riding* hood? Was she riding a horse?"

"Maybe she had a horse that she rode sometimes. But not in this story. Now stop interrupting every minute."

Annemarie smiled, feeling her way through the dark, remembering how Kirsti always interrupted stories to ask questions. Often she just wanted to make the story last longer.

The story continued. "One day the little girl's mother said, 'I want you to take a basket of food to your grandmother. She is sick in bed. Come, let me tie your red cloak.'"

"The grandmother lived deep in the woods, didn't she?" Kirsti would ask. "In the dangerous woods, where wolves lived."

Annemarie heard a small noise—a squirrel perhaps, or a rabbit, scampering nearby. She paused, stood still on the path, and smiled again. Kirsti would have been frightened. She would have grabbed Annemarie's hand and said, "A wolf!" But Annemarie knew that these woods were not like the woods in the story. There were no wolves or bears or tigers, none of the beasts that populated Kirsti's vivid imagination. She hurried on.

Still, they were very dark, these woods. Annemarie had never followed this path in the dark before. She had told her mother she would run. And she tried.

Here the path turned. She knew the turning well, though it seemed different in the dark. If she turned to the left, it would take her to the road, out where it would be lighter, wider, more traveled. But more dangerous, too. Someone could see her on the road. At this time of dawn, other fishermen would be on the road, hurrying to their boats for the long day at sea. And there might be soldiers.

She turned to the right and headed deeper into the woods. It was why Mama and Peter had needed to guide those who were strangers here—the Rosens and the others. A wrong turn would have taken them into danger.

"So little Red Riding-Hood carried the basket of food and hurried along through the woods. It was a lovely morning, and birds were singing. Little Red Riding-Hood sang, too, as she walked."

Sometimes she changed that part of the story, telling it to Kirsti. Sometimes it was raining, or even snowing, in the woods. Sometimes it was evening, with long, frightening shadows, so that Kirsti, listening, would snuggle closer and wrap her arms around Annemarie. But now, telling it to herself, she wanted sunlight and bird song.

Here the path widened and flattened; it was the place where the woods opened on one side and the path curved beside a meadow at the edge of the sea. Here she could run, and she did. Here, in daylight, there would be cows in the meadow, and on summer afternoons Annemarie would always stop by the fence and hold out handfuls of grass, which the curious cows would take with their rough tongues.

Here, her mother had told her, Mama would always stop, too, as a child walking to school. Her dog, Trofast, would wriggle under the fence and run about in the meadow, barking excitedly, trying to chase the cows, who always ignored him.

The meadow was empty now, and colorless in the half light. She could hear the churning sea beyond, and see the wash of daylight to the east, over Sweden. She ran as fast as she could, searching with her eyes for the place ahead where the path would re-enter the woods in its final segment, which led to town.

Here. The bushes were overgrown and it was difficult to see the path here. But she found the entrance, beside the high blueberry bushes—how often she had stopped here, in late summer, to pick a handful of the sweet berries! Her hands and mouth would be blue afterward; Mama always laughed when she came home.

Now it was dark again, as the trees and bushes closed around her, and she had to move more slowly, though she still tried to run.

Annemarie thought of Mama: her ankle so swollen, and her face so pained. She hoped Mama had called the doctor by now. The local doctor was an old man, brusque and businesslike, though with kind eyes. He had come to the farmhouse several times during the summers of the past, his battered car noisy on the dirt road; he had come once when Kirsti, a tiny baby then, had been sick and wailing with an earache. And he had come when Lise had spilled hot grease, cooking breakfast, and burned her hand.

Annemarie turned again as the path divided once more. The left fork would take her directly to the village; it was the way they had come from the train, and the way Mama had walked to school as a girl. But Annemarie turned to the right, heading now toward the harborside, where the fishing boats lay at anchor. She had often come this way before, too, sometimes at the end of the afternoon, to pick

out the *Ingeborg*, Uncle Henrik's boat, from the many returning, and
to watch him and his helpers unload the day's catch of slippery,
shimmering herring still flopping in their containers.

Even now, with the boats in the harbor ahead empty of fish,
preparing to leave for the day's fishing, she could smell the oily, salty
scent of herring, which always remained in the air here.

It wasn't far now, and it was getting lighter. She ran almost as fast
as she had run at school, in the Friday footraces. Almost as fast as she
had run down the Copenhagen sidewalk on the day that the soldier
had stopped her with his call of "*Halte!*"

Annemarie continued the story in her head. "Suddenly, as Little
Red Riding-Hood walked through the woods, she heard a noise. She
heard a rustling in the bushes."

"A wolf," Kirsti would always say, shivering with fearful delight.
"I know it's going to be the wolf!"

Annemarie always tried to prolong this part, to build up the
suspense and tantalize her sister. "She didn't know *what* it was. She
stopped on the path and listened. Something was following her, in
the bushes. Little Red Riding-Hood was very, very, *very* frightened."

She would stop, would stay silent for a moment, and beside her
in the bed she could feel Kirsti holding her breath.

"Then," Annemarie would go on, in a low, dread-filled voice, "she
heard a *growl*."

Annemarie stopped, suddenly, and stood still on the path. There
was a turn immediately ahead. Beyond it, she knew, as soon as she
rounded the turn, she would see the landscape open to the sea. The
woods would be behind her there, and ahead of her would be the harbor,
the docks, and the countless fishing boats. Very soon it would be
noisy there, with engines starting, fishermen calling to one another,
and gulls crying.

But she had heard something else. She heard bushes rustling
ahead. She heard footsteps. And—she was certain it was not her
imagination—she heard a low growl.

Cautiously, she took a step forward. And another. She approached
the turn in the path, and the noises continued.

Then they were there, in front to of her. Four armed soldiers.
With them, straining at taut leashes, were two large dogs, their eyes
glittering, their lips curled.

Chapter 15 | My Dogs Smell Meat!

$\mathbf{A}$NNEMARIE'S MIND RACED. She remembered what her mother had said. "If anyone stops you, you must pretend to be nothing more than a silly little girl."

She stared at the soldiers. She remembered how she had stared at the others, frightened, when they had stopped her on the street.

Kirsti hadn't been frightened. Kirsti had been—well, nothing more than a silly little girl, angered because the soldier had touched her hair that afternoon. She had known nothing of danger, and the soldier had been amused by her.

Annemarie willed herself, with all her being, to behave as Kirsti would.

"Good morning," she said carefully to the soldiers.

They looked her up and down in silence. Both dogs were tense and alert. The two soldiers who held the leashes wore thick gloves.

"What are you doing here?" one of them asked.

Annemarie held out her basket, with the thick loaf of bread visible. "My Uncle Henrik forgot his lunch, and I'm taking it to him. He's a fisherman."

The soldiers were looking around; their eyes glanced behind her, and scanned the bushes on either side.

"Are you alone?" one asked.

Annemarie nodded. "Yes," she said. One of the dogs growled. But she noticed that both dogs were looking at the lunch basket.

One soldier stepped forward. The other, and the two holding the dogs, remained where they were.

"You came out before daybreak just to bring a lunch? Why doesn't your uncle eat fish?"

What would Kirsti reply? Annemarie tried to giggle, the way her sister might. "Uncle Henrik doesn't even *like* fish," she said, laughing. "He says he sees too much of it, and *smells* too much of it. Anyway, he wouldn't eat it raw!" She made a face. "Well, I suppose he would if he were starving. But Uncle Henrik always has bread and cheese for lunch."

Keep chattering, she told herself, as Kirsti would. A silly little girl. "I like fish," she went on. "I like it the way my mother cooks it. Sometimes she rolls it in bread crumbs, and—"

The soldier reached forward and grabbed the crisp loaf of bread from the basket. He examined it carefully. Then he broke it in half, pulling the two halves apart with his fists.

That would enrage Kirsti, she knew. "*Don't!*" she said angrily. "That's Uncle Henrik's bread! My mother baked it!"

The soldier ignored her. He tossed the two halves of the loaf to the ground, one half in front of each dog. They consumed it, each snapping at the bread and gulping it so that it was gone in an instant.

"Have you seen anyone in the woods?" The soldier barked the question at her.

"No. Only you." Annemarie stared at him. "What are you doing in the woods, anyway? You're making me late. Uncle Henrik's boat will leave before I get there with his lunch. Or what's *left* of his lunch."

The soldier picked up the wedge of cheese. He turned it over in his hand. He turned to the three behind him and asked them something in their own language.

One of them answered "*Nein,*" in a bored tone. Annemarie recognized the word; the man had replied "No." He had probably been asked, Annemarie thought, "Do you want this?" or perhaps, "Should I give this to the dogs?"

The soldier continued to hold the cheese. He tossed it back and forth between his hands.

Annemarie gave an exasperated sigh. "Could I go now, please?" she asked impatiently.

The soldier reached for the apple. He noted its brown spots, and made a face of disgust.

"No meat?" he asked, glancing at the basket and the napkin that lay in its bottom.

Annemarie gave him a withering look. "You know we have no meat," she said insolently. "Your army eats all of Denmark's meat."

Please, please, she implored in her mind. Don't lift the napkin.

The soldier laughed. He dropped the bruised apple on the ground. One of the dogs leaned forward, pulling at his leash, sniffed the apple, and stepped back. But both dogs still looked intently at the basket, their ears alert, their mouths open. Saliva glistened on their smooth pink gums.

"My dogs smell meat," the soldier said.

"They smell squirrels in the woods," Annemarie responded. "You should take them hunting."

The soldier reached forward with the cheese in one hand, as if he were going to return it to the basket. But he didn't. Instead, he pulled out the flowered cotton napkin.

Annemarie froze.

"Your uncle has a pretty little lunch," the soldier said scornfully, crumpling the napkin around the cheese in his hand. "Like a woman," he added, with contempt.

Then his eyes locked on the basket. He handed the cheese and napkin to the soldier beside him.

"What's that? There, in the bottom?" he asked in a different, tenser voice.

What would Kirsti do? Annemarie stamped her foot. Suddenly, to her own surprise, she began to cry. "I don't know!" she said, her voice choked. "My mother's going to be angry that you stopped me and made me late. And you've completely ruined Uncle Henrik's lunch, so now *he'll* be mad at me, too!"

The dogs whined and struggled against the leashes, nosing forward to the basket. One of the other soldiers mutter something in German.

The soldier took out the packet. "Why was this so carefully hidden?" he snapped.

Annemarie wiped her eyes on the sleeve of her sweater. "It wasn't hidden, any more than the napkin was. I didn't know what it is." That, she realized, was true. She had no idea what was in the packet.

The soldier tore the paper open while below him, on the ground, the dogs strained and snarled, pulling against their leashes. Their muscles were visible beneath the sleek, short-haired flesh.

He looked inside, then glared at Annemarie. "Stop crying, you idiot girl," he said harshly. "Your stupid mother has sent your uncle a handkerchief. In Germany the women have better things to do. They don't stay at home hemming handkerchiefs for their men."

He gestured with the folded white cloth and gave a short, caustic laugh. "At least she didn't stitch flowers on it."

He flung it to the ground, still half wrapped in paper, beside the apple. The dogs lunged, sniffed at it eagerly, then subsided, disappointed again.

"Go on," the soldier said. He dropped the cheese and the napkin back into her basket. "Go on to your uncle and tell him the German dogs enjoyed his bread."

All of the soldiers pushed past her. One of them laughed, and they spoke to each other in their own language. In a moment they had disappeared down the path, in the direction from which Annemarie had just come.

Quickly she picked up the apple and the opened packet with the white handkerchief inside. She put them into the basket and ran around the bend toward the harbor, where the morning sky was now bright with early sun and some of the boat engines were starting their strident din.

The *Ingeborg* was still there, by the dock, and Uncle Henrik was there, his light hair windblown and bright as he knelt by the nets. Annemarie called to him and he came to the side, his face worried when he recognized her on the dock.

She handed the basket across. "Mama sent your lunch," she said, her voice quavering. "But soldiers stopped me, and they took your bread." She didn't dare to tell him more.

Henrik glanced quickly into the basket. She could see the look of relief on his face, and knew that it was because he saw that the packet was there, even though it was torn open.

"Thank you," he said, and the relief was evident in his voice.

Annemarie looked quickly around the familiar small boat. She could see down the passageway into the empty cabin. There was no sign of the Rosens or the others. Uncle Henrik followed her eyes and her puzzled look.

"All is well," he said softly. "Don't worry. Everything is all right."

"I wasn't sure," he said. "But now"—he eyed the basket in his hands—"because of you, Annemarie, everything is all right.

"You run home now, and tell your mama not to worry. I will see you this evening."

He grinned at her suddenly. "They took my bread, eh?" he said. "I hope they choke on it."

I Will Tell You Just a Little

Chapter 16

Poor Blossom!" Uncle Henrik said, laughing, after dinner that evening. "It was bad enough that your mother was going to milk her, after all these years of city life. But Annemarie! To do it for the very first time! I'm surprised Blossom didn't kick you!"

Mama laughed, too. She sat in a comfortable chair that Uncle Henrik had moved from the living room and placed in a corner of the kitchen. Her leg, in a clean white cast to the knee, was on a footstool.

Annemarie didn't mind their laughing. It *had* been funny. When she had arrived back at the farmhouse—she had run along the road to avoid the soldiers who might still be in the woods; now, carrying nothing, she was in no danger—Mama and Kirsti were gone. There was a note, hastily written, from Mama, that the doctor was taking her in his car to the local hospital, that they would be back soon.

But the noise from Blossom, forgotten, unmilked, uncomfortable, in the barn, had sent Annemarie warily out with the milking bucket. She had done her best, trying to ignore Blossom's irritated snorts and tossing head, remembering how Uncle Henrik's hands had worked with a firm, rhythmic, pulling motion. And she had milked.

"I could have done it," Kirsti announced. "You only have to pull and it squirts out. I could do it *easily*."

Annemarie rolled her eyes. I'd like to see you try, she thought.

"Is Ellen coming back?" Kirsti asked, forgetting the cow after a moment. "She said she'd make a dress for my doll."

"Annemarie and I will help you make a dress," Mama told her. "Ellen had to go with her parents. Wasn't that a nice surprise, that the Rosens came last night to get her?"

"She should have waked me up to say goodbye," Kirsti grumbled, spooning some imaginary food into the painted mouth of the doll she had propped in a chair beside her.

"Annemarie," Uncle Henrik said, getting up from the table and pushing back his chair, "if you come with me now to the barn, I'll give you a milking lesson. Wash your hands first."

"Me too," said Kirsti.

"Not you too," Mama said. "Not this time. I need your help here, since I can't walk very well. You'll have to be my nurse."

Kirsti hesitated, deciding whether to argue. Then she said, "I'm going to be a nurse when I grow up. Not a cow milker. So I have to stay here and take care of Mama."

Followed as usual by the kitten, Annemarie walked with Uncle Henrik to the barn through a fine misty rain that had begun to fall. It seemed to her that Blossom shook her head happily when she saw Henrik and knew that she would be in good hands again.

She sat on the stacked hay and watched while he milked. But her mind was not on the milking.

"Uncle Henrik," she asked, "Where are the Rosens and the others? I thought you were taking them to Sweden on your boat. But they weren't there."

"They were there," he told her, leaning forward against the cow's broad side. "You shouldn't know this. You remember that I told you it was safer not to know.

"But," he went on, as his hands moved with their sure and practiced motion, "I will tell you just a little, because you were so very brave."

"Brave?" Annemarie asked, surprised. "No, I wasn't. I was very frightened."

"You risked your life."

"But I didn't even think about that! I was only thinking of—"

He interrupted her, smiling. "That's all that *brave* means—not thinking about the dangers. Just thinking about what you must do. Of course you were frightened. I was too, today. But you kept your mind on what you had to do. So did I. Now let me tell you about the Rosens.

"Many of the fishermen have built hidden places in their boats. I have, too. Down underneath. I have only to lift the boards in the right place, and there is room to hide a few people. Peter, and others in the Resistance who work with him, bring them to me, and to the other fishermen as well. There are people who hide them and help them, along the way to Gilleleje."

Annemarie was startled. "Peter is in the Resistance? Of course! I should have known! He brings Mama and Papa the secret newspaper, *De Frei Danske*. And he always seems to be on the move. I should have figured it out myself!"

"He is a very, very brave young man," Uncle Henrik said. "They all are."

Annemarie frowned, remember the empty boat that morning. "Were the Rosens and the others there, then, underneath, when I brought the basket?"

Uncle Henrik nodded.

"I heard nothing," Annemarie said.

"Of course not. They had to be absolutely quiet for many hours. The baby was drugged so that it wouldn't wake and cry."

"Could they hear me when I talked to you?"

"Yes. Your friend Ellen told me, later, that they heard you. And they heard the soldiers who came to search the boat."

Annemarie's eyes widened. "Soldiers came?" she asked. "I thought they went the other way after they stopped me."

"There are many soldiers in Gilleleje and all along the coast. They are searching all the boats now. They know that the Jews are escaping, but they are not sure how, and they rarely find them. The hiding places are carefully concealed, and often we pile dead fish on the deck as well. They hate getting their shiny boots dirtied!"

He turned his head toward her and grinned.

Annemarie remembered the shiny boots confronting her on the dark path.

"Uncle Henrik," she said, "I'm sure you are right, that I shouldn't know everything. But, please, would you tell me about the handkerchief? I knew it was important, the packet, and that's why I ran through the woods to take it to you. But I thought maybe it was a map. How could a handkerchief be important?"

He set the filled pail aside and began to wash the cow's udder with the damp cloth. "Very few people know about this, Annemarie," he said with a serious look. "But the soldiers are so angry about the escaping Jews—and the fact that they can't find them—that they have just started using trained dogs."

"They had dogs! The ones who stopped me on the path!"

Uncle Henrik nodded. "The dogs are trained to sniff about and find where people are hidden. It happened just yesterday on two boats. Those damn dogs, they go right through dead fish to the human scent.

"We were all very, very worried. We thought it meant the end of the escape to Sweden by boat.

"It was Peter who took the problem to scientists and doctors. Some very fine minds have worked night and day, trying to find a solution.

"And they have created a special drug. I don't know what it is. But it was in the handkerchief. It attracts the dogs, but when they sniff at it, it ruins their sense of smell. Imagine that!"

Annemarie remembered how the dogs had lunged at the handker-chief, smelled it, and then turned away.

"Now, thanks to Peter, we will each have such a handkerchief, each boat captain. When the soldiers board our boats, we will simply pull the handkerchiefs out of our pockets. The Germans will probably think we have bad colds! The dogs will sniff about, sniff the handker-chiefs we are holding, and then roam the boat and find nothing. They will smell nothing."

"Did they bring dogs to your boat this morning?"

"Yes. Not twenty minutes after you had gone. I was about to pull away from the dock when the soldiers appeared and ordered me to halt. They came aboard, searched, found nothing. By then, of course, I had the handkerchief. If I had not, well—" His voice trailed off, and he didn't finish the sentence. He didn't need to.

If she had not found the packet where Mr. Rosen had dropped it. If she had not run through the woods. If the soldiers had taken the basket. If she had not reached the boat in time. All of the ifs whirled in Annemarie's head.

"They are safe in Sweden now?" she asked. "You're sure?"

Uncle Henrik stood, and patted the cow's head. "I saw them ashore. There were people waiting to take them to shelter. They are quite safe there."

"But what if the Nazis invade Sweden? Will the Rosens have to run away again?"

"That won't happen. For reasons of their own, the Nazis want Sweden to remain free. It is very complicated."

Annemarie's thoughts turned to her friends, hiding under the deck of the *Ingeborg*. "It must have been awful for them, so many hours there," she murmured. "Was it dark in the hiding place?"

"Dark, and cold, and very cramped. And Mrs. Rosen was seasick, even though we were not on the water very long—it is a short distance, as you know. But they are courageous people. And none of that mattered when they stepped ashore. The air was fresh and cool in Sweden; the wind was blowing. The baby was beginning to wake as I said goodbye to them."

"I wonder if I will ever see Ellen again," Annemarie said sadly.

"You will, little one. You saved her life, after all. Someday you will find her again. Someday the war will end," Uncle Henrik said. "All wars do.

"Now then," he added, stretching, "that was quite a milking lesson, was it not?"

"Uncle Henrik!" Annemarie shrieked, and then began to laugh. "Look!" She pointed. "The God of Thunder has fallen into the milk pail!"

Chapter 17 | All This Long Time

THE WAR WOULD END. Uncle Henrik had said that, and it was true. The war ended almost two long years later. Annemarie was twelve.

Churchbells rang all over Copenhagen, early that May evening. The Danish flag was raised everywhere. People stood in the streets and wept as they sang the national anthem of Denmark.

Annemarie stood on the balcony of the apartment with her parents and sister, and watched. Up and down the street, and across on the other side, she could see flags and banners in almost every window. She knew that many of those apartments were empty. For nearly two years, now, neighbors had tended the plants and dusted the furniture and polished the candlesticks for the Jews who had fled. Her mother had done so for the Rosens.

"It is what friends do," Mama had said.

Now neighbors had entered each unoccupied, waiting apartment, opened a window, and hung a symbol of freedom there.

This evening, Mrs. Johansen's face was wet with tears. Kirsti, waving a small flag, sang; her blue eyes were bright. Even Kirsti was growing up; no longer was she a lighthearted chatterbox of a child. Now she was taller, more serious, and very thin. She looked like the pictures of Lise at seven, in the old album.

Peter Neilsen was dead. It was a painful fact to recall on this day when there was so much joy in Denmark. But Annemarie forced herself to think of her redheaded almost-brother, and how devastating the day was when they received the news that Peter had been captured and executed by the Germans in the public square at Ryvangen, in Copenhagen.

He had written a letter to them from prison the night before he was shot. It had said simply that he loved them, that he was not afraid, and that he was proud to have done what he could for his country and for the sake of all free people. He had asked, in the letter, to be buried beside Lise.

But even that was not to be for Peter. The Nazis refused to return the bodies of the young men they shot at Ryvangen. They simply buried them there where they were killed, and marked the graves only with numbers.

Later, Annemarie had gone to the place with her parents and they had laid flowers, on the bleak, numbered ground. That night, Annemarie's parents told her the truth about Lise's death at the beginning of the war.

"She was part of the Resistance, too," Papa had explained. "Part of the group that fought for our country in whatever ways they could."

"We didn't know," Mama added. "She didn't tell us. Peter told us after she died."

"Oh, Papa!" Annemarie cried. "Mama! They didn't shoot Lise, did they? The way they did Peter, in the public square, with people watching?" She wanted to know, wanted to know it all, but wasn't certain that she could bear the knowledge.

But Papa shook his head. "She was with Peter and others in a cellar where they held secret meetings to make plans. Somehow the Nazis found out, and they raided the place that evening. They all ran different ways, trying to escape."

"Some of them *were* shot," Mama told her sadly. "Peter was shot, in the arm. Do you remember that Peter's arm was bandaged, and in a sling, at Lise's funeral? He wore a coat over it so that no one would notice. And a hat, to hide his red hair. The Nazis were looking for him."

Annemarie didn't remember. She hadn't noticed. The whole day had been a blur of grief. "But what about Lise?" She asked. "If she wasn't shot, what happened?"

"From the military car, they saw her running, and simply ran her down."

"So it was true, what you said, that she was hit by a car."

"It was true," Papa told her.

"They were all so young," Mama said, shaking her head. She blinked, closed her eyes for a moment, and took a long, deep breath. "So very, very young. With so much hope."

Now, remembering Lise, Annemarie looked from the balcony down into the street. She saw that below, amid the music, singing, and the sound of churchbells, people were dancing. It brought back another memory, the memory of Lise so long ago, wearing the yellow dress, dancing with Peter on the night that they announced their engagement.

She turned and went to her bedroom, where the blue trunk still stood in the corner, as it had all these years. Opening it, Annemarie saw that the yellow dress had begun to fade; it was discolored at the edges where it had lain so long in folds.

Carefully she spread open the skirt of the dress and found the place where Ellen's necklace lay hidden in the pocket. The little Star of David still gleamed gold.

"Papa?" she said, returning to the balcony, where her father was standing with the others, watching the rejoicing crowd. She opened her hand and showed him the necklace. "Can you fix this? I have kept it all this long time. It was Ellen's."

Her father took it from her and examined the broken clasp. "Yes," he said. "I can fix it. When the Rosens come home, you can give it back to Ellen."

"Until then," Annemarie told him, "I will wear it myself."

Afterword

HOW MUCH OF ANNEMARIE'S story is true? I know I will be asked that. Let me try to tell you, here, where fact ends and fiction begins.

Annemarie Johansen is a child of my imagination, though she grew there from the stories told to me by my friend Annelise Platt, to whom this book is dedicated, who was herself a child in Copenhagen during the long years of the German occupation.

I had always been fascinated and moved by Annelise's descriptions not only of the personal deprivation that her family and their neighbors suffered during those years, and the sacrifices they made, but even more by the greater picture she drew for me of the courage and integrity of the Danish people under the leadership of the king they loved so much, Christian X.

So I created little Annemarie and her family, set them down in a Copenhagen apartment on a street where I have walked myself, and imagined their life there against the real events of 1943.

Denmark surrendered to Germany in 1940, it is true; and it was true for the reasons that Papa explained to Annemarie: the country was small and undefended, with no army of any size. The people would have been destroyed had they tried to defend themselves against the huge German forces. So—surely with great sorrow—King Christian surrendered, and overnight the soldiers moved in. From then on, for five years, they occupied the country. Visible on almost every street corner, always armed and spit-shined, they controlled the newspapers, the rail system, the government, schools, and hospitals, and the day-to-day existence of the Danish people.

But they never controlled King Christian. It is true that he rode alone on his horse from the palace every morning, unguarded, and greeted his people; and though it seems so charming as to be a flight of author's fancy, the story that Papa told Annemarie, of the soldier who asked the Danish teenager, "Who is that man?"—that story is recorded in one of the documents that still remain from that time.

It is true, too, that in August 1943 the Danes sank their own entire navy in Copenhagen harbor as the Germans approached to take over the ships for their own use. My friend Annelise remembers it, and many who were children at the time would have been awakened, as little Kirsti was, by the explosions and the fiercely lighted sky as the ships burned.

On the New Year of the Jewish High Holidays in 1943, those who gathered to worship at the synagogue in Copenhagen, as the fictional Rosens did, were warned by the rabbi that they were to be taken and "relocated" by the Germans.

The rabbi knew because a high German official told the Danish government, which passed the information along to the leaders of the Jewish community. The name of that German was G.F. Duckwitz, and I hope that even today, so many years later, there are flowers on his grave, because he was a man of compassion and courage.

And so the Jews, all but a few who didn't believe the warning, fled the first raids. They fled into the arms of the Danes who took them in, fed them, clothed them, hid them, and helped them along to safety in Sweden.

In the weeks following the Jewish New Year, almost the entire Jewish population of Denmark—nearly seven thousand people—was smuggled across the sea to Sweden.

The little hand-hemmed linen handkerchief that Annemarie carried to her uncle? Surely something made up by an author who wanted to create a heroine out of a fictional little girl?

No. The handkerchief as well is part of history. After the Nazis began to use police dogs to sniff out hidden passengers on the fishing boats, Swedish scientists worked swiftly to prevent such detection. They created a powerful powder composed of dried rabbit's blood and cocaine; the blood attracted the dogs, and when they sniffed at it, the cocaine numbed their noses and destroyed, temporarily, their sense of smell. Almost every boat captain used such a permeated handkerchief, and many lives were saved by the device.

The secret operations that saved the Jews were orchestrated by the Danish Resistance, which, like all Resistance movements, was composed mainly of the very young and very brave. Peter Neilsen, though he is fictional, represents those courageous and idealistic young people, so many of whom died at the hands of the enemy.

In reading of the Resistance leaders in Denmark, I came across an account of a young man named Kim Malthe-Bruun, who was eventually captured and executed by the Nazis when he was only twenty-one years old. I read his story as I had read many others, turning the pages, skimming here and there: this sabotage, that tactic, this capture, that escape. After a while even courage becomes routine to the reader.

Then, quite unprepared, I turned the page and faced a photograph of Kim Malthe-Bruun. He wore a turtleneck sweater, and his thick, light hair was windblown. His eyes looked out at me, unwavering on the page.

Seeing him there, so terribly young, broke my heart. But seeing the quiet determination in his boyish eyes made me determined, too, to tell his story, and that of all the Danish people who shared his dreams.

So I would like to end this with a paragraph written by that young man, in a letter to his mother, the night before he was put to death.

> . . . and I want you all to remember—that you must not dream yourselves back to the times before the war, but the dream for you all, young and old, must be to create an idea of human decency, and not a narrow-minded and prejudiced one. That is the great gift our country hungers for, something every little peasant boy can look forward to, and with pleasure feel he is a part of—something he can work and fight for.

Surely that gift—the gift of a world of human decency—is the one that all countries hunger for still. I hope that this story of Denmark, and its people, will remind us all that such a world is possible.

Related Readings

Jean-Louis Besson   from *October '45: Childhood Memories of the War*   personal narrative   **85**

Harold Gordon   **Night of Fire at Berlin Railroad Station**   personal narrative   **90**

Garrison Keillor   **Civilized Denmark**   essay   **96**

Sasha Whyte   **We Will Be the World**   magazine article   **106**

Henry Roth   **Petey and Yotsee and Mario, July 14, 1956**   short story   **109**

Jean-Louis Besson

from
October '45: Childhood Memories of the War

In the following reading, Jean-Louis Besson describes daily life in Paris, France, during World War II. Besson was seven years old at the time, and his experience of the war is quite different from Ellen Rosen's. As you read, think about the different ways World War II affected both Besson's and Rosen's lives.

June '40

The Invasion

June. The Germans are here! No one thought they would arrive so quickly. The war is no longer a phony war. Tears stream down Uncle Albert's face as he watches the Germans pass in front of the store, in perfect formation, on their motorbikes and in their trucks. He says, "When I think how hard we fought during the other war . . . We would never have let them get this far!"

The Beginning of the Occupation

Two German officers visited the doctor today to ask permission to stay in his house—only in the guest room, so as not to bother anyone. They speak French very well. The doctor says they're very proper, for enemies.

At Uncle Albert's, Miss Leduby, the grocer, tells us that a German soldier came into her store this morning. This one didn't speak French, but when he pointed to a jar sitting on the counter, she understood that he wanted one of the wrapped confections[1] that were inside. Since he didn't have any money to pay, she gave it to him. He unwrapped the gold paper, put the confection in his mouth and immediately started yelling "Oh! Oh!" in German before running out of the store. It was a concentrated bouillon cube,[2] which made us all laugh. But everyone agrees that the German soldiers seem well disciplined. We certainly won't be finding them on the streets at night making a drunken racket like the English.

Two weeks later we see Papa way at the end of the road that leads to the clinic. He's carrying a little suitcase in his hand. We've been worried about him; we've had no news from him because the mail isn't operating. He traveled any way he could from Pamiers—hitchhiking, on carts, by train sometimes, and often on foot. His shoes have holes in them. He no longer has socks, but the puttees[3] held up. For him the war is over. France has asked for an armistice.[4] In other words, our country has promised not to fight anymore. We're so happy to have Papa back with us!

July '40

Life Begins Again

It's summer again and school is out. The rural police passed through the streets today and, after a drum roll, informed the population that all orders would now be coming from the German kommandantur,[5] now located next to the town hall in the old castle of the city. The first order: curfew at 9:00 P.M. Everyone must go home, and all lights must be out. As for Uncle Albert's pigeons, they are no longer allowed to fly over the city, probably for fear they'll transport secret messages. At least they weren't confiscated.[6]

---

1. **confections** candies
2. **bouillon cube** meat extract used to make soup
3. **puttees** leggings
4. **armistice** temporary cease-fire by mutual consent
5. **kommandantur** headquarters
6. **confiscated** taken and kept

Uncle Albert now travels by bicycle to farmers' homes to repair the separators, the machines that separate the cream from the milk and make butter. Many people are also bringing him sewing machines now, since there are rarely any new clothes in the stores. Aunt Reine still serves cider in her café, and Mama, behind her counter, still sends letters and packages, sometimes to Germany for the prisoners. . . .

June '41

An exhibition

. . . Small posters have appeared in the windows of certain stores that say "Jewish Establishment." You see them often in the windows of the many clothing and shoe stores in Belleville. This is, no doubt, to tell us to avoid going there. Of course we don't pay any attention. We know all the shopkeepers in our neighborhood and we like them. In any case, there is less and less merchandise for sale, and everyone says it's not good quality.

These days, most shoes have wooden soles that clatter when you walk. Others have cork or split plywood soles that bend, but everyone says they're not sturdy. Uncle Gaston gives us an old tire from his car, which my father cuts into pieces to nail to the bottoms of our shoes. It makes the soles stronger.

The ladies complain that they can't buy any stockings. My three cousins in Montreuil, who are very elegant, tint their legs with walnut stain from the paint store and then draw false seams on them with a pencil. They say that all their friends do the same. It's very pretty, but of course it doesn't keep them warm.

People are having trouble finding clothes, and yet sometimes you see strange young people, the zazous, who have started a new style of wearing incredible outfits. Jackets that are way too big over short, narrow trousers, ties as narrow as strings, hats pushed back and shoes with enormous soles. They always have umbrellas in their hands, especially when the weather is nice. The girls have bouffant[7] hairdos, enormous hats, and skirts that don't even reach their knees.

---

7. **bouffant** full, puffed out

July '41

Supplies

The main problem we face is finding food. In the German system you need tickets to buy everything. Everyone has a food card, with different categories depending on one's age, from J1 for babies to V for the elderly. My sister and I are J2, which gives us the right to more bread, milk, and meat than the adults. When we reach sixteen we'll be J3, unless of course the war ends before then.

We are constantly waiting in line at the stores, especially if they sell products that don't require tickets, like leeks or potatoes. Often the wait is very long and Mother asks us to stand in line for her. The folding chair has become a necessity. One thing you can always buy, though, is rutabagas. You don't need a ticket and you don't have to wait in line to buy them, either, because they're not very good. They're big turnips that are ordinarily used to feed animals in the country.

We've found that you can make all sorts of dishes with potatoes, even cake if you have a little flour. Instead of coffee we grill barley. We call that an ersatz, which is a German word that means substitute. Tobacco is also rationed and smokers make cigarettes out of mint or eucalyptus leaves, or with flower petals. But no one in our house smokes.

There is also the black market. You can buy anything there if you have the money. My friend Pignel, the son of the eyeglass merchant, tells me that every week his parents buy a big fat steak. It's expensive, of course, but very good. Aunt Odette has a friend, Mr. Peyronnet, who works at police headquarters with the Germans and who brings her gifts from time to time—a bottle of oil or a leg of lamb—hidden in a newspaper. She speaks of him in a hushed voice.

Fortunately, Aunt Reine, who still lives in Vitré, never fails to send us a package whenever she can. She always includes a chicken or rabbit, butter, and lard. Enough to get by. From time to time, we also get a pigeon.

In the summer, on Sundays when the weather is good, we take the train to the country with all our picnic baskets and gather mulberries in the bushes. They make a good inexpensive dessert for no tickets. We could also gather mushrooms, but my parents say it's too dangerous, that we might pick the wrong ones and get a stomachache, or worse. . . .

August '41

Family Life

. . .We finally have a wireless set at home. My father had always refused to buy one, saying that it was too expensive and that all you heard was garbage, but now we need to listen to the English broadcast like everyone else. It's forbidden by the government, of course, and we have to adjust the sound very low, just as everyone else does, because of neighbors who might turn us in.

Every evening the program begins with four slightly mysterious, muffled sounds: "Boom, boom, boom, boom," and then, "From London, the French speak to the French." You really have to make an effort to listen because of the static, and also because the program disappears completely at certain moments. They say that the war is far from over and that the Germans will end up losing. And there's a French general in London whom no one has ever heard of—General de Gaulle—who is calling on people to continue to fight on the side of the English. But here no one really believes that together we could win the war.

Paris by Night

At night the city turns completely black. According to the curfew, as soon as evening falls, no light may shine from any house, not even the slightest glow from the edge of a curtain. The cracks in the shutters have all been plugged up with newspapers or pieces of rag. The lamps are covered with blue paint that is just barely transparent, as are the headlights of the few cars. With bicycles and cars it's all right to leave a narrow crack to let a little light shine through.

This doesn't stop anyone from visiting friends. All you have to do is carry a flashlight, also painted blue, quickly turning it on in case you encounter an obstacle, and return home before eleven to avoid running into the booted steps of a patrol.

Harold Gordon

Night of Fire at Berlin Railroad Station

from
The Last Sunrise: A True Story

Harold Gordon was born in 1931 in Grodno, Poland, and was sent to a Nazi concentration camp at the age of ten. Following is a chapter from his book, which he wrote more than fifty-two years later, describing his experiences during World War II.

I HAD NOT YET REACHED MY FOURTEENTH BIRTHDAY. Another empty cattle train eased itself through the gates of Auschwitz to the very same landing spur[1] where we had first arrived about a year before. The doors of the dirty, old cattle train slid open, as it had many times before. Each car was packed to capacity with prisoners. After the transport was completely loaded without incident, the doors slid shut, locked and sealed as if they were carrying precious cargo. These sealed doors would not be reopened under any circumstances until we arrived at our destination. We were already too weak, both mentally and physically, to care. We knew from experience that an existence worse than death was awaiting us for the next several days. We were to be without food, water, or sanitation facilities. Not one of us knew where we were going or why.

---

1. **spur** branch of railroad track

The train traveled very slowly for several hours as if the locomotive couldn't get up enough steam for the heavy load it was pulling. It might have even been going up a grade. We were gasping for air in the heated car and didn't care about our ultimate destination. We felt that this time none of us would be alive when the doors to our cars would finally slide open. The locomotive quit pulling and we felt the train slowing again. It came to a halt at a remote side track waiting for more important trains to pass, trains filled with wounded German soldiers returning from the Russian front and munition trains heading north to resupply the German army.

It was late in the afternoon. The temperature in the locked cattle car was very high. The two small windows did not provide enough air for the occupants to breathe. We had been sitting there motionless for six hours. At least when we were in motion, the cooler air from outside would seep in through the cracks and we would get some relief. We felt that dying would be a blessing for us, ending our suffering. I felt that I was going to die soon anyway and postponing the inevitable would be much more painful in the long run.

Just as our death wish was about to come true, the train began moving again and the temperature began to fall. It was early evening. It was cooling off outside and cooler air entering through the crack was of great benefit. We traveled all through the night and a second day. On the third night, our train eased itself slowly into a very large railroad station. We heard many trains coming and going as our train proceeded to a side spur. I saw the platform and a sign with the station name through the crack in the door. The lit sign read "**BERLIN.**" We all became very excited when we realized that we were inside Germany. The train came to a halt. Each one of us came up with his own version of why we were there. The train continued moving very slowly, switching tracks for almost half an hour until it finally came to a halt at the most remote track of the Berlin railroad station, where we would probably spend the night for one reason or another. We felt a jerk as the locomotive disconnected and abandoned us on the side track.

It wasn't long after we stopped that we heard explosions in the night, and through the cracks in the door I saw many fires erupting all around the railroad station. German soldiers were running around in confusion and firemen attempted to put out the fires. Explosions erupted more frequently and many trains were on fire all around us. Through the cracks we saw wounded German soldiers, some of them on fire. Munitions trains were exploding all around us, adding to the chaos. The train next to us was on fire. We could feel the additional heat from the burning train next to us, through the walls of our box car. The German guards left the scene and abandoned us in the locked box cars. I knew that soon our train would be hit and would ignite like all the other trains around us. The bombs continued hitting their mark, causing one explosion right after another. Steel and wooden objects were flying through the air, igniting other trains, and puncturing cars as they landed. We didn't care so much about dying at the hands of the Allies, but we didn't want to die in the gas chamber. Within fifteen minutes, which seemed like an eternity, the bombing had stopped and everything around us was burning. Shells were still exploding from the burning munitions trains. The danger had not yet passed for us. We could still be hit by exploding shells or catch on fire from the burning train on the adjoining track. By some miracle, our train was spared from the bombs and did not ignite from the surrounding fires.

We realized that the railroad station was being bombed by the Allies. (We learned later that the British bombed by night while the Americans bombed by day.) At first we were frightened and aware that we were locked in a train which could ignite at any moment. This was not the way we would have chosen to die. I felt that since death was just around the corner, I would rather die by allied bombs than at the hands of the Germans.

The next morning, our locomotive was sent to remove some of the burned cars to clear the main track. It took two more days to repair the damaged tracks. Our black, smoke-puffing locomotive returned to us at the end of the second day and hooked on to our train with a big jolt. We began moving again and a few hours later we arrived at a new railroad station. The sign said "**Oraninburg**".

It was raining as we unloaded the train. We had to march two miles to our new camp. We could barely walk. The short distance we had to walk seemed like an eternity. We collected raindrops in our folded hands for drinking and the wetness that covered our bodies was refreshing. Some of us who could no longer walk were left in the box cars and the rest of us proceeded to the main gates of the "Katzet Lager" (KZ).

As we passed through the main gates, we found ourselves inside a fenced camp with modern barracks, well-paved streets and sidewalks.

It looked like a well-organized army base. There was a lot of activity on the streets. Army trucks rushed by us on the rain-drenched street, spraying us as they drove by. We were led in a column down the main street. The weaker people fell behind and were disposed of later, just like the ones who couldn't leave the train station. The SS guards wore rainproof pants, ponchos, and boots and were in good physical condition. They looked superhuman to us. Maybe it was because we felt so weak and inferior at that time. We were all led into what looked like a large empty hangar with only straw on the floor. About two thousand of us were packed into this one large hangar which was to be our home.

Each prisoner selected a small spot on the thin straw to make his home. My father told me to stay where I was. He was going to gather some more straw for us to sleep on. A few minutes later I saw a Nazi guard kicking and beating someone on the ground about fifty or so feet from where I was sitting. I did not move from my designated space for fear that my dad might never find me. He had been gone a long time and I was beginning to worry that he might not return. A while later, Dad returned. I told him what I saw; he did not comment.

We were put to work almost immediately doing garbage detail and cleaning up the streets. Once a day we'd get our moldy bread rations and a bowl of thin, tasteless soup that looked more like dirty dish water than soup. This became our routine. A few days later, after work, as we were sitting on the straw in the hangar, my dad took off his shirt. I noticed black and blue marks all over his upper body. I asked him, "Where did you get the marks?" He told me that it was he who had been beaten up a few days before while looking for extra straw in the dim light of evening. A strange feeling came over me. I thought to myself, I saw my own dad being beaten and didn't even know it. I felt very bad and scared. My dad was my hero—being beaten and not being able to defend himself was mentally destructive to what little hope and confidence was still left in my being.

Head count was at 5:00 A.M. every morning. We had less than six minutes to get dressed and out the door. We had to sleep with our clothes on because of the cold and also because it took too long to get dressed in the morning. Some of our work also consisted of digging ditches and carrying bricks or sacks of sand or cement on our backs. Every time the sirens sounded because of the Allies' air raids (twice a day), we'd be rushed to our hangar. After the all-clear siren was sounded, we'd go back to what we had been doing.

We heard many airplanes taking off and landing and I felt that we were near an air base. At night, in the hangar, during the air raids, I kept listening to the sound of the Allied bombers approaching. It was predictable. Almost every night, we heard sirens and then the faint sounds of approaching aircraft. I was one of the first to hear the sound of the heavy, loaded bombers because I was the youngest and my ears were probably better than most. I wished that I could go outside and wave and shout, "drop your bombs here so we might have a chance to escape." But of course our doors were shut and locked for the night. As the airplane engines became faint in the distance, the all-clear sirens sounded once more. We knew that the sirens would not remain silent for very long because Berlin was only about thirty miles away and we knew as well as the Germans that Berlin was the squadrons' destination, where the bombs were to be released. The Allied planes would return over our camp again on the way back to England, empty of bombs. The sound of the unloaded B-17 bomber was different, of higher pitch. We could tell by the sound of the engines that the bomb load was dropped successfully. I don't recall any German fighters going up to challenge the Allied bombers, even though we were right on top of a Messerschmitt[2] aircraft factory.

This became a daily routine. It got so that I could tell in an instant which direction the planes were headed by the sound of the engines. I often thought, what if the pilots couldn't drop all of their bombs on Berlin and decided to drop the remaining load on the hangars that were our home? It looked so much like an airplane hangar. We would be destroyed instantly.

I heard a few anti aircraft batteries open fire at the overhead Allied squadron and I don't recall them ever scoring a hit. After the daytime air raids when we were allowed outside and looked at the sky, I could see the black rings of smoke high in the sky created by the anti aircraft shells exploding. This went on for three weeks. Every day the routine was the same. The bombers would come, drop the bombs over Berlin, and return empty to England.

One particular Sunday, things were different. Allied planes approached Oraninburg as usual, and as usual the sirens sounded and

---

2. **Messerschmitt** the most common German fighter airplane of World War II

anti aircraft fire was sent up. The all-clear siren sounded a few minutes later and we knew from past experience that within one hour the sirens would sound again as the empty planes returned on their way back to England after the bombing run on Berlin. This time when the empty planes approached overhead, the engines sounded different. The sound was low, as under a heavy load. Their engines had the characteristic of high rpm,[3] laboring, hard working, under a heavy load. I told my father that something was different this time. Suddenly, to our total surprise, the B-17s began dropping their bomb load at a corner of our camp—to be more precise, on a young pine forest recently planted. Beneath the ground was a modern, well-camouflaged Messerschmitt plane factory. Bombs exploded nearby and there was total chaos[4] among the Germans. The airplane factory was destroyed, including all the Messerschmitt planes below. The airfield was also destroyed in the same raid. Within minutes, there was total and complete destruction of the entire facility.[5] We found pleasure in knowing that the Allies knew where the airplane factory was located—not at the obvious hangars where the prisoners slept, but beneath the ground under a pine forest. None of the hangar barracks was even slightly damaged; not a single prisoner was hurt. After that, there was no more reason for us to remain here, so we were shipped out on yet another train.

3. **rpm** revolutions per minute
4. **chaos** great confusion
5. **facility** building that serves a particular purpose

Garrison Keillor

Civilized Denmark

Humorist Garrison Keillor is a well-known author and radio talk-show host. A frequent visitor to Denmark, Keillor explains his affection for the country and offers his own description of the Danish people and their culture.

DENMARK is a little land of five and a quarter million souls, most of them Andersens, Hansens, Jensens, Jacobsens, or Petersens, with a few Madsens and Mortensens and Rasmussens thrown in for variety, who live on a pleasant green peninsula and two large islands and many tiny ones north of Germany, between the North Sea and the Baltic, a major supplier of ham and cheese and ceramics, a nation of irreligious Lutherans, a democratic society prickly to wealth and privilege and the home of a royal line that goes back to A.D. 935. The peninsula is Jutland; the two islands are Zealand, which includes Copenhagen, and Fyn. A handsome and civilized country, its only wilderness the sea.

The entire country is a little smaller than Lake Michigan, and if it were slipped in there, between Wisconsin and Michigan, it would not be such a bad fit culturally. The same dark humor prevails as in the Midwest, the same stoicism[1] and gentility.[2] It would be a shock to land in a Great Lake, but the Danes would study the situation and work out the best deal they could, keeping their queen and flag, their chirpy language, their generous health and unemployment benefits, their 37-hour work week, their five weeks of annual vacation plus assorted holidays, their nine political parties (Social Democrats on the

---

1. **stoicism** calm acceptance of fate
2. **gentility** courtesy

left, Radikale in the center, Venstre, or Left, on the right). They might ban the so-called Danish pastry (too gooey). They would make fun of everything American and lambaste[3] our foreign policy. They would see themselves, in every way, as the beautiful swan trapped in the realm of ducks.

Life in Denmark is divided into two parts, the Golden Summer and the Great Murk, which extends from late fall to mid-spring. The months of youth and beauty, when the sky is light until almost 11 P.M. and Danes take to the beaches, eat in their gardens, soak up the sun, feel sleek and smart, and the other months, when they go to and from work in the dark and the rain and just try to keep putting one foot in front of the other and not get too glum.

I used to spend Christmases in Denmark, back when I had connections there, and I remember the night flight over the Atlantic, the sun rising to reveal the solid cloud bank below, the descent through cloud to Copenhagen Airport, like coal miners going down into the hole, the pilot putting the wheels down and the ground still not visible, and then, suddenly, red-tile roofs of houses in the mist below, deep green meadows, tree lines, rain trickling across the window, and the wheels bump on the runway, and you're in Denmark, in a gloom so dense you feel it in your skull.

You disembark onto a shopping concourse, and past the mink coats and crystal a sign points you to customs. You parade through, a little surprised at how casually the Danish police glance at your passport. (The man who waves you in may be the last uniform you'll see for a while, Danes being a self-policing people who prefer that authority be inconspicuous.[4]) You collect your bags, and off to the cabstand, the air gray, drizzly, with a tang of salt and smoke.

The cab races off through Amager, past the soccer fields and into the streets of the city, the identical brown-brick apartment buildings, the mustard stucco houses, passing a stream of bicyclists pedaling solemnly to work in their bright red or yellow slickers. Danish jumps out at you from signs, lots of cognates[5] here: A drugstore is an *apotek* (remember apothecary), and a merchant is a *handler*—a *boghandler* sells books, a *vinhandler* wine—a *restaurant* is a restaurant, and you realize that you won't starve here or get lost.

---

3. **lambaste** verbally attack
4. **inconspicuous** hard to notice
5. **cognate** a word related to one in another language

Sober-faced Danes queue[6] at the bus stop in the rain, which they do not flinch at, and it dawns on you that a daylong rain is not unusual, this is a North Atlantic winter. The sun won't shine tomorrow, maybe not the next day. You have arrived in a land where Christmas means more than in, say, Barbados; it is the last outpost on the long grim trek toward spring. Dark gray sky at noon, dull brown brick all around, dead trees, broken glass in the gutter, and you, sorry you, your head like a sponge full of mud. At first you think it's jet lag, and then you realize that everyone else feels this way too. Welcome to the birthplace of existentialism.[7]

The taxi brings you over the canal and into the heart of Copenhagen, the grand old city that has resisted freeway and highrise in defense of its narrow, twisting brick streets from medieval times, its skyline of green church steeples, its pretty squares and fountains. Past the Christiansborg Castle where parliament sits, past the big department store, Magasin, and the Royal Theater hulking on Kongens Nytorv, a plaza faced by stately old piles,[8] and up a narrow street called Bredgade (Broad Street), past the queen's palace at Amalienborg, and up to Østerbro, where I once lived, in a big echoey belle epoque[9] apartment on Trondhjemsgade. The dining room had a 14-foot ceiling with plaster moldings, and when I sat in it, writing, it felt as if I were drafting the Treaty of Ghent.

We celebrated Juleaften there every December 24. My stepchildren and I trudged through the late afternoon mists to Trinitatis Kirke, where little Søren Kierkegaard[10] attended confirmation class, the church the Round Tower is attached to. It was packed to the rafters Christmas Eve with shiny children and their *mors* and *fars* and *mormors* and *morfars* and *farmors* and *farfars*. We sang the old Danish carols and heard a sermon about our obligations to the Third World and hiked home to our pork roast and caramelized potatoes, and the oldest boy lit the candles on the tree in the dining room and threw the doors open, and we looked at it and gasped—every year the same

---

6. **queue** line up

7. **existentialism** twentieth-century thought emphasizing that individuals are responsible for what they make of themselves

8. **piles** supporting foundation posts

9. **belle epoque** belonging to a period of high artistic and cultural development in late nineteenth-century France

10. **Søren Kierkegaard** nineteenth-century Danish philosopher

gasp—and ran hand in hand through the dark rooms singing, "*Nu er det jul igen,*" and opened our gifts.

The 25th is an afterthought, a quiet day for recuperation; Christmas Eve is the great night of the year. And on Nytårsaften, the 31st, you sit down at 6 P.M., along with everyone else in Denmark, and watch Queen Margrethe deliver her annual homily[11] to the people. It lasts about 12 minutes and ends with her greetings to the people of Greenland and the Faroe Islands and to the people who work on the sea. "Heart-felt greetings from the prince and me," she says, beaming. "God bless Denmark.". . . At midnight Danish television plays the romantic national anthem, and you stand, champagne in hand, and sing it, reading the words off the screen. At 2 A.M., to clear your head, you go for a walk. Blocks and blocks of five-story brick houses; gray, white, cream, blue, gold candles flickering in the casement windows; the steep red- or black-tile roofs, the forest of chimneys, dormers in the garrets; and you feel the romance of Copenhagen, as if walking into an old painting, the enchantment of darkness and rain and the warm hearth that you eventually will walk back to.

I had seen enough Danish Decembers to hold me for a while, so I flew over last year in June for a week of summer. I looked around Århus, the handsome harbor city with a forest next to its downtown. . . .

I drove up to Skagen, where the turn-of-the-century artists Michael and Anna Ancher and P. S. Krøyer painted fishermen and garden parties and ladies in white strolling along a beach under the midnight sun. I took the train to Fyn for Midsummer Eve. I visited Gilleleje, the vacation village on the north coast of Zealand from which, to escape the Germans in October 1943, Danish Jews were smuggled by fishing boat over the sound to Sweden. . . .

And I hiked around Copenhagen, along earthworks and remains of moats and along the pier where cruise ships tie up, to the statue of the Little Mermaid, sitting on her rock, looking small and forlorn, and beyond her to the magnificent fountain of Gefion, the goddess at the plow, lashing her oxen, water spraying from their nostrils, and great plumes arching up from the plowshare. I sat at outdoor cafés in

---

11. **homily** inspirational speech

Gråbrødretorv and Kultorvet and spoke my pitiful rusty Danish to waiters and ate my herring and studied the passersby. Danes are good to watch. They keep a stolid public expression, like Buster Keaton, and are masters of the raised eyebrow. Let a waiter drop a tray of dishes and looks of deadpan[12] amusement flicker on every face, including the waiter's. I step into a bakery, and when the girl behind the counter says, "Goddag," I say, "Goddag, jeg vil gerne ha' to lille stykke boller," and her left brow lifts and she says, "Oh, you want two of these buns?" "Ja, tak," I say. "You speak Danish well," she says. "Where in America are you from?" . . . .

It is—let's be frank here—almost everyone's idea of the World's Most Nearly Perfect Nation: a clean, peaceful, well-regulated society populated by prosperous (but not greedy or rapacious), tolerant (but principled), law-abiding (but humorous), computer-literate, bi- or trilingual people who all vote in elections and are as witty as Victor Borge[13] . . . and reside in sunny, energy-efficient homes, the decor running toward light woods and primary colors, who can discuss (in excellent English) the infrastructure[14] needs of developing countries or the Danishness of Woody Allen while serving perfectly poached salmon off handsome earthenware, copies of which are on display at the Museum of Modern Art in New York City.

Despite Denmark's manifest virtues, Danes never talk about how proud they are to be Danes. This would sound weird in Danish and violate their pride of modesty. When Danes talk to foreigners about Denmark, they always begin by commenting on its tininess, its unimportance, the difficulty of its language, the general small-mindedness and narcissism[15] and self-indulgence of their countrymen, the high taxes—52 percent is the average income tax rate, and there's a 25 percent sales tax. No Dane would look you in the eye and say, "Denmark is a great country." You are supposed to figure this out for yourself.

It is the land of the silk safety net, where almost half the national budget goes toward smoothing out life's inequalities, and there is plenty of money for schools, day care, retraining programs, job

---

12. **deadpan** expressionless
13. **Victor Borge** twentieth-century Danish musician and comedian
14. **infrastructure** basic framework
15. **narcissism** love of self

seminars—Danes love seminars: Three days at a study center hearing about waste management is almost as good as a ski trip. It is a culture bombarded by English, in advertising, pop music, movies, the Internet, all the chic media, and despite all the English that Danish absorbs—there is no Danish Academy to defend against it—old dialects persist in Jutland that can barely be understood by Copenhageners. It is the land where, as the saying goes, "Few have too much and fewer have too little," and an American is struck by the sweet egalitarianism[16] that prevails, where the lowliest clerk gives you a level gaze, where Sir and Madame have disappeared from common usage, even Mr. and Mrs., and children address teachers by their first names. It's a nation of recyclers—about 55 percent of Danish garbage gets made into something new—and no nuclear power plants: The Danes prefer windmills. It's a nation of tireless planners. Trains run on time. Things operate well in general. Only 2 percent of the national budget goes to police and prisons and courts, and 3 percent to defense. It is a famously peace-loving country, whose troops, part of the UN peacekeeping force in Bosnia, engaged Serbian militia in a firefight in April 1994, the first official Danish act of war since 1864. . . .

Nonetheless, it is an orderly land. You drive through a Danish town, it comes to an end at a stone wall, and on the other side is a field of barley, a nice clean line: town here, country there. The stores close at six, even earlier on Saturday, and on Sunday you window-shop; an American has to learn that sometimes you just plain can't have it. It is not a nation of jaywalkers. People stand on the curb and wait for the red light to change, even if it's 2 A.M. and there's not a car in sight. The red light is part of the system: You cross against it, and you are showing disdain for your countrymen. (I feel sheepish[17] waiting for the red light, so I cross, and several times I discovered that Danish drivers don't slow down for jaywalkers. They don't see you in the crosswalk because you're not supposed to be there.)

Danes don't think of themselves as a waiting-at-2-A.M.-for-the-green-light people—that's how they see Swedes and Germans. Danes see themselves as a jazzy people, improvisers, more free spirited than Swedes, but the truth is (though one should not say it) that Danes are

---

16. **egalitarianism** belief in human equality
17. **sheepish** embarrassed

very much like Germans and Swedes. Orderliness is a main selling point. Denmark has few natural resources, limited manufacturing capability; its future in Europe will be as a broker, banker, and distributor of goods. You send your widgets by container ship to Copenhagen, and these bright, young, English-speaking, utterly honest, highly disciplined people will get your widgets around to Scandinavia, the Baltic States, and Russia. Airports, seaports, highways, and rail lines are ultramodern and well-maintained. There is a presumption of punctuality here. An American train leaves the station if all the members of the Departure Committee can find no reason for it to wait; the Danish train leaves the station unless someone throws himself across the track and he happens to be someone they like.

Daily life turns on predictability. If the time table says that the train leaves Klampenborg at 7:06 and arrives at Østerport Station at 7:27, those times are reliable, and if you invite Jens and Camilla for dinner at 7:30, that's exactly when they'll knock on your door, not two minutes later. And when you open the door, they will expect that you too have managed your time and are not racing around snatching up dirty socks, that dinner is under control, the candles lit, the wine chilling, the hosts prepared to be congenial. . . .

The orderliness of the society doesn't mean that Danish lives are less messy or lonely or angst-ridden[18] than yours or mine, and no Dane would tell you so. You can hear plenty about bitter family feuds and the sorrows of alcoholism and about aimless, overindulged young people working the system to make a cushy life for themselves and perfectly sensible people who went off one day and killed themselves. An orderly society can't exempt its members from the hazards of life.

But there is a sense of entitlement and security that Danes grow up with and Americans don't. Certain things are yours by virtue of citizenship, and everyone knows what they are, they're the same for everyone, and you shouldn't feel bad for taking what you're entitled to, you're as good as anyone else. A woman in Hørsholm, who had lived in California as a child, told me: "I miss people I knew in America, how open and friendly they were, but it's better to have a safety net under you. You might not have a chance to do big things, but nothing so bad will happen to you." The rules of the welfare system are clear to everyone, the benefits you get if you lose your job, the

---

18. **angst-ridden** filled with feelings of anxiety or insecurity

steps you take to get a new one; and the orderliness of the system makes it possible for the country to weather high unemployment and social unrest without a sense of crisis.

There is social unrest in the World's Cleanest and Most Organized Country—which is, to an American, certainly interesting, considering how Danes once lectured us about racial intolerance, but never mind that. Now you hear them discuss the country's troubles with its Yugoslavian and Turkish guest workers, who came 30 years ago when the country needed cheap labor, and today the guest workers' children, Danish-born, Danish-speaking, Muslim, are discriminated against because they have the wrong last names. Protest demonstrations flare up in the Muslim ghettos of Ishøj, and right-wing politicians have seized on the issue. But I never heard the problem described as intractable: Everybody seemed to think it would get worked out eventually.

Denmark is the stable society it is because it is productive and prosperous, and because Danes get a similar start in life, whether you grow up in the mansions of Hellerup or the tenements of Nørrebro. At birth you become a member of the Lutheran Church. (You can petition to get out, but it's no simple matter.) You go to similar day care centers, toddle off to the same kindergartens, then to a *folkeskole* for grades one to nine, where, in the fourth grade, you begin the serious study of English (in seventh, German or French). There isn't Public School 10 for the poor and St. Cuthbert's-on-the-Hill for the mill owner's children; everybody goes down the same road. In the spring of ninth grade you reach the great divide and find out if you go to *gymnasium* or a technical school or a business school for late bloomers. Gymnasium is for the serious student, no troublemakers, no slackers, no goofballs. About 40 percent wind up there. At the same time the state starts paying you a stipend of up to 1,800 kroner[19] a month ($260), depending on your parents' income. It's meant to even up the odds a little more.

After three years of gymnasium you take the test that pretty much decides your career, the *studenter* exam. Admission to various colleges and professional schools is by bidding, high studenter scores get first dibs. It takes a very high score to get into the humanities, medicine, dentistry, or psychology—a lesser score to major in math or physics or chemistry or theology . . .

---

19. **kroner** Danish currency

My last day in Denmark I took the Inter-City Express from Copenhagen to the island of Fyn for Midsummer Eve at the house of old friends, a teacher and his wife, a writer. The train no longer switches onto a ferry for the trip across the Great Belt; it slips into a tunnel and races under the sea and up to an island and over a bridge, the longest rail-auto bridge in Europe, 6.6 kilometers long, one of a series of bridge and tunnel links that will knit Denmark together and tie the country to Sweden. My friends, Britt and Torben, met me at the station, and we drove south to their house.

I said I missed the train-ferry, and they said they had mixed feelings about it. "But then we Danes love to hold two opposing views at the same time," said Britt. "That's probably why there was no referendum on the bridges, because the people might have voted against them out of sentiment, even though everyone knows they're necessary. We can't think of ourselves as an island anymore. But we still do."

The car wheeled south, through the rolling paradise of Fyn, and we talked about the Danish love of paradox[20]—the tendency to strive to get ahead and deny that you are doing any such thing. To belong to the Lutheran Church and yet never attend except at Christmas. ("Actually," said Britt, "attendance is up a little. You see 14-year-olds coming in to be baptized, sometimes over their parents' objections. Anyway, there are more coming in than going out.") The paradox of a highly secular[21] society—no Dane running for office need make any public show of religious faith whatsoever, in fact it would be taken as bad taste—and yet Danes take Easter as a holiday and Maundy Thursday and Good Friday and Easter Monday, plus three days for Christmas, and Whitmonday, and something called Great Prayer Day in April. "Well, that's just us," said Britt.

Danes have belonged to the European Union since 1973 and still, down deep, feel opposed to it, she said. "We are terribly offended by our bureaucrats[22] who go to Brussels to work for the EU and earn more than their counterparts here, fly first-class, live in luxury apartments—at least, we think they're luxurious. We're funny that way. If 90 Danes were living the high life in Brussels, or if we thought they were, we might very well vote Denmark out of it."

---

20. **paradox** a statement that seems to contradict itself
21. **secular** not related to religion
22. **bureaucrats** government officials

Britt and Torben's house is an 18th-century stone house on the outside, modern on the inside, old casement windows with thermal panes, an antique ship captain's table with a computer on it, by which Torben exchanges e-mail with me. Shelves full of books, dozens of American novels, Cheever, Updike, Hemingway, Paul Auster. The house looks down a long slope of meadow toward the sea, the island of Langeland in the distance, and the island of Ærø, the name of which I am one of the few living Americans to pronounce almost correctly, they told me. I was so proud, I tried to work Ærø into the conversation all evening. Even if I barely understood what the conversation was about, I said, "Would this also be true on Ærø?"

There were 30 guests milling around in the backyard when I arrived, and a few minutes later we took our seats at two long tables in the backyard. Torben raised his glass and welcomed everyone and said, "Skål. Velkommen." And we sat down to shrimp salad and poached salmon and lamb and red wine and very good bread.

The dinner included long toasts, to the queen and to America and to one another, and there were songs about the beauty of the Danish landscape and Hans Christian Andersen's hymn that begins, "In Denmark was I born, there I have a home; there is my root, from there my world begins. O you Danish tongue, you are my mother's voice, how sweetly you bless my heart." Every time I looked around, I saw people smiling.

Sasha Whyte

We Will Be the World

In the following article, Sasha Whyte describes her trip to Bosnia in southeast Europe. At the time, Bosnia was plagued by fighting between different ethnic groups. Whyte took the trip as part of an after-school journalism program.

MOSTAR IN BOSNIA means "old bridge." It is also a small city in southern Bosnia, famous for its Turkish bridges built from the 1400s. These bridges were a symbol for the city and gave it its name and tradition. A little more than a month ago, I was in Mostar on one of the old bridges with Alem Prguda, a kid from the eastern side of the city. His eyes fixed on the green river below, Alem recited his story as if he had told it many times before. He was 12 when his Mostar home was shelled by the Croats. His youngest brother went to go look at a bird flying outside his window. He got hit by a grenade and died. That was the saddest day of Alem's life.

I met Alem on a 10-day, UNICEF-sponsored trip through the former Yugoslavia. I lived at his house for two days and at another Mostar family's home for two more. Alem's mother asked me about my mother, how many children she had. I told her I was an only child. She asked me if my mother smoked cigarettes, which I thought was strange. I told her my mother didn't smoke. She nodded and told me she never smoked until her son was killed. Then she took out pictures of her two young sons before the war. Alem's father made a dismissive motion with his hands and told her to stop. Alem looked really solemn, as if he wanted to leave the room. But his mother insisted on showing me the pictures. She wanted me to see the son she lost in the war.

A few days later a French UNICEF worker told me that when a mother loses her child, part of her dies and she can never recover.

Only then did it hit me that a part of Alem's mother had died along with her son. She had the look that I was to see many times in Mostar, a look so far off and distant, you wondered if the person was still alive. It made me wonder if people can survive without a soul. It also made me angry that nothing was accomplished by the war and that nothing has ever been accomplished by war.

As an American, aside from Sally Struthers and her tearful appeals to help kids, suffering was a remote concept to me. I chose to ignore the various conflicts around the globe, figuring they had no importance to my life as a New York City high-school sophomore.

When I heard I was going to Bosnia with Children's Express News Service, the after-school journalism program I work for, the thought of what a war-torn country would be like didn't really occur to me. It was my beginning assignment as a foreign correspondent and I was excited about going to Europe for the first time. Even the people I told downplayed the seriousness of it all. Some teachers and adults patted me on the back and told me how this trip would help my college essay. My friends cracked jokes about Croatia Airlines and told me I would finally meet people thinner than myself.

I prepared for my trip like a journalist: studying maps, reading articles and writing many questions. But when we got there most of my questions were useless. They were too broad and had to do more with what we would see, rather than what we did see in the former Yugoslavia.

As we were driving toward Mostar, I fell asleep with the Adriatic coast outside my window. I woke up an hour later to see buildings covered with bullet holes and soldiers walking through the streets. I couldn't tell the difference between the holes from shells and grenades until a UNICEF worker explained that a shell mark is like a spiral and a grenade mark is just a hole.

To me, everything just looked like Swiss cheese. And I always smelled something burning. It was really the smell of burning garbage, but it had symbolic meaning. It was like being in the aftermath of something really big, and you just wanted to keep asking everybody what happened.

Electricity and water have been restored in Mostar, which is now divided into Croat and Muslim sections like Berlin after World War II. Kids on both sides go to school, watch TV, eat dinner and try to lead regular lives. But many of these kids have lost brothers, sisters and their entire families. How can their lives ever be normal?

In Mostar West, the Croatian side, I interviewed a kid named Goran Bevanda, who told me that things would be better only when the next generation came along. "We are the destroyed generation now," he said. A lot of the adults we interviewed kept telling us that the children were not bitter and that they were the key to peace in the Mostar of the future. I saw another side—that the children were not ready to forgive and forget.

I sat in on a Bosnian chemistry class. The teacher talked on the subject while the kids appeared bored and sat drawing pictures. Everybody smoked in the school halls. You figure that students really had the need to smoke and the teachers understand why. . . .

A lot of younger kids were born during the war. They have no thought of what their lives would be like without war, so they're conditioned by it. If you were to slam a door they would jump a mile. They hear firecrackers at night and wonder who it is this time. A lot of the boys are into firecrackers. A few kids tried to sell me firecrackers because they wanted to see my reaction. I was always surprised. Some of them had lost their homes. Some had lost family and they still wanted to play war. But I guess in that way they were like normal boys.

Before going to Bosnia I thought the kids would be different from American kids. But the scary thing is, they weren't. It shows that war can happen anywhere and touch anybody. Everyone always says the point of remembering the Holocaust is to make sure it won't happen again, but after talking to kids in the former Yugoslavia, I learned how easily it can happen again.

Henry Roth

Petey and Yotsee and Mario, July 14, 1956

Henry Roth moved to the United States from Austria-Hungary in 1908. His family first settled in New York City's Lower East Side and then moved to Harlem a few years later. In this short story, Roth talks about learning to accept his own cultural heritage.

THERE WAS A DOCK that stretched out into the Harlem River at about 130th Street, a few blocks north of the New York Central and New Haven station; the trestle[1] of the railroad crossed the river only a short distance from where we swam. To the west was the Madison Avenue turn bridge, and across the river were the freight yards and a large lumberyard. Below us, the big bucket of a coal company crane pounded monotonously into the hold of a scow[2] and issued dripping lumps of coal. Tugs wallowed[3] by, solitary sometimes, or towing barges, their bow mats like brown mustaches over foam. We went in when the tide was high; the water looked cleaner then and covered the mud flats. We sat on the torrid,[4] splintery dock and slipped into our trunks—tights, we called them—and dived off.

---

1. **trestle** bridge
2. **scow** large, flat-bottomed boat
3. **wallowed** rolled
4. **torrid** scorchingly hot

I had just learned to swim that summer, and was already considered a fair swimmer, though nothing in comparison with Petey and Yotsee and Mario, who were there from my block. They swam with a special Sunday stroke, an overhand that slapped the water with a kind of strict flip of the wrist, and they kept their chests above the surface. I hadn't mastered that yet.

One day, I swam out into the river. It looked inviting. And whether the changing tide pulled me out farther than I realized or I allowed myself to be lured out farther, I don't know, but when I turned back, I found myself at a considerable distance from the dock, and also found that I was tired. And then the inevitable unforeseen happened: a passing tug sent a following wave over me that left me gasping and gagging. I tried to regulate my breathing again and move those leaden arms. But if I was gaining on the dock, it wasn't apparent; it seemed in motion itself, away from me. And now the rebound from the original wave slapped me in the face, and I was really beginning to flounder. Consciousness became an alternation between glimpses of sunlight on weathered dock and somewhat longer glimpses of pale-green water. I heard the cry go up from the dock: "Hey, Fat's drownin'!"

They came splashing toward me, all three of them—Petey and Yotsee and Mario.

"I'm all right," I gasped when they reached me. I could feel hands under me as I labored forward. I could hear their laughter. They towed me in toward the dock, swimming on their backs and screaming with laughter. And then they gave me a final shove toward the slimy piles and I climbed up the makeshift ladder. I sat panting on the dock while they climbed, too. "Gee, I must have been drowning," I said.

"You musta been," Petey said.

"You wasn't drownin'. You was just fetchin' way down," Yotsee said.

"He wasn't drownin'," said Mario. "He was just tryin' to dive to the bottom and run like hell for the shore!"

And, overcome with mirth,[5] they bellywhopped off the dock.

When I got home, I told my mother and my sister what had happened.

"Thank God!" said my mother. "Blessed Gentile children to save you! May the Almighty bestow[6] on them that joy they bestow on me!"

---

5. **mirth** laughter, delight
6. **bestow** give

"You're a dope to go out so far," said my sister.

"I didn't know I was out that far," I protested.

"Why didn't you look back?"

"I know," said my mother. "I'm going to bake them a cake."

"What?"

"I'm going to bake them a cake. Now. A big one." She was already clearing a space on the covered washtubs for her earthenware mixing bowl.

"Aw, Mom," I said. "That ain't what—" I couldn't express it. "Don't bake them no cake."

"Why not?"

"Aw, you bake Jewish cakes."

"And what kind of cakes are not Jewish cakes?"

"Oh, you know. Like in the store. Ward's. Tip-Top. Golden Queen. Like that."

"Go, go," she said. "I'll bake them a spicecake."

"It's Jewish."

"Don't be a fool," said my mother.

She baked them a spicecake. It was embossed[7] with walnuts, dark with crystallized honey, and full of raisins—our typical holiday spicecake.

"Well," she said, exhibiting it when it had cooled. "Who needs to be ashamed of this? Will you give it to them or not?"

"Aw, Mom, they don't understand cakes like that."

"Are they in the street?"

"Yes."

"Then come with me." She slipped the cake carefully into a paper bag, and I followed her reluctantly down the stairs and into the street. "Where are they?"

"There. There's Petey—with the handball. There's Yotsee. Mario is by the cellar. Those three."

"Come."

I trailed her across the street. The three boys were lolling[8] in front of the candy store, just east of the corner.

"You, Petey. You, Mario," she said, and they lifted their tough lean faces.

---

7. **embossed** decorated with raised figures
8. **lolling** lounging

"And what is the other's name?" she asked, turning to me.

"Yotsee. Yotsee Hunt."

"And you. Yotsee. You should be blessed for saving my son."

"Oh," Petey said. They understood.

"That's nothin'," Yotsee said.

"Fat's—I mean, he's from the block." Mario sent his finger through a curve of explanation.

"You—If I could talk better," she said, "I would tell you. You all got mamas. They understand. Sometime you ask them, they'll explain you."

"Aw, we won't tell 'em. What's the difference?" said Yotsee.

"Here's from me a cake."

They stared at her. "For us?" Petey asked.

"It's for you. You should remember."

They took it from her—Petey took it. "Thanks," he said.

"You're welcome," my mother said.

I followed her back to the stoop, and there we stood a little while, watching them. Petey was brandishing[9] the cake aloft. "Hey, Weasel! Look!" The rest of the gang converged on them. We could hear their avid[10] cries: "What about us?" "Hey, what about a hunk?" The cake was broken and divided and eaten with gusto.[11] Still munching, Mario pointed us out. My mother nodded in acknowledgment.

"You see?" She turned to me. "What were you afraid of?"

"I don't know."

"You were afraid they wouldn't like Jewish cake. What kind of people would they be if they didn't like Jewish cake? Would they have even saved you?" she said, and went into the house.

---

9. **brandishing** waving about

10. **avid** eager

11. **gusto** enthusiasm